She put both of her hands behind my neck and roughly pulled me down so she could kiss me. Her mouth was urgent, insistent on mine, and I responded. I'd forgotten, after all the years, how good her mouth tasted, how sweet her breath was. Suddenly my mouth was on her neck and we were undressing each other eagerly.

"The bedroom?" I asked.

"No," she said, "here, on the floor."

"Mandy—" I began . . . and she silenced me with a deep, probing kiss. Her breasts blossomed into my hands . . . .

Don't miss any of the lusty, hard-riding action in the new Charter Western series, THE GUNSMITH:

And coming next month:

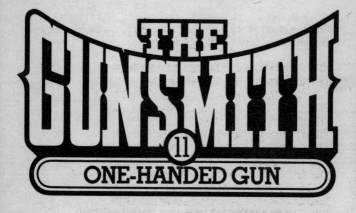

THE GUNSMITH

11

ONE-HANDED GUN

J.R. ROBERTS

CHARTER BOOKS, NEW YORK

THE GUNSMITH #11: ONE-HANDED GUN

A Charter Book / published by arrangement with
the author

PRINTING HISTORY
Charter Original / November 1982
Second printing / June 1983

ISBN: 0-441-30866-X

Charter Books are published by The Berkley Publishing Group,
200 Madison Avenue, New York, N.Y. 10016.
PRINTED IN THE UNITED STATES OF AMERICA

Dedication

To my son, Christopher,
who is always on the
lookout for my copies

THE GUNSMITH #11
ONE-HANDED GUN

PROLOGUE

July 1873

Palmerville, Wyoming had never been anything but a quiet town filled with quiet, law-abiding people. Recently, in its quiet way, the town had been becoming more and more prosperous. The last time anyone could remember the Palmerville bank being robbed was in 1858, when One-eyed Billy Nelson had been refused a loan of ten dollars, and went in with a shotgun, stealing thirty and leaving town without hurting anyone, never to be seen again.

Just fifteen years later, however, there was considerably more money in the Palmerville bank than there had ever been before—and the Bucket brothers knew it.

Ethan and Clem Bucket had lived in Palmerville for all of their respective twenty-one and twenty-three years. Their pa, Nathaniel Bucket, had been an overbearing father and had kept the boys tied to their failing ranch for years, but now Nathaniel was dead, struck down by a heart attack at fifty-three, and the Buckets knew that it was time to leave. All they needed was a little cash.

Clem was the brains, and he told Ethan, "You

stay outside by the horses and I'll go in and get the money."

"Why can't I come in?" Ethan asked.

Now Clem didn't want his younger brother inside the bank because Ethan thought he was Jesse James. Clem didn't want Ethan to shoot anybody inside the bank. Robbing a bank wasn't much, but killing somebody, that'd have the law tracking you forever.

Clem didn't tell his brother this, though.

"Look, Ethan, we need somebody out here as a lookout, and to hold the horses—and you know you're much better with horses than I am," Clem explained.

"That's true," Ethan said, accepting the explanation.

"Okay," Clem said, "I'm gonna go inside now."

"How much we gonna get, Clem?" Ethan asked his older brother.

"I'm gonna get as much as I can, Ethan," Clem said, "and then we are gonna leave this town behind us for good."

Ethan smiled broadly at his brother and then assumed his stern, Jesse James look, which he had been practicing all night. Clem shook his head and went into the bank.

He walked up to the teller's window and said, "Cora, this here's a holdup."

The bucktoothed young girl behind the window stared at him and then said, "Go on, Clem Bucket," but stopped when Clem took out his pa's beaten up .45 and pointed it at her.

"This ain't no joke, Cora," he said. "Gimme the money."

"Oh, my God," the young teller said, "Oh, my God."

"Cora, just put the money in some kinda bag and give it to me," Clem commanded.

"Oh, my God," she said again.

"Look out," Clem said, impatiently, pushing her away. He hoisted himself up and through the window onto the other side.

It was early in the morning and there were no customers in the Palmerville bank yet, but Mr. Hawthorne, the bank manager, was there, and he saw what was happening.

"Hey," he shouted, "what are you doing? You can't do that!"

Clem pointed the .45 at Mr. Hawthorne and cocked the hammer, which shut the older man up.

"You just keep quiet, Mr. Hawthorne, and you won't get hurt. I'm robbing your bank."

"What?" the manager asked. "You're what? This bank hasn't been robbed in years!"

"Then it's high time, I say," Clem replied. "Now shut up and let me get on with it." He began looking around behind the window, and then said, "Damn it, don't you have any sacks around here?"

When no one answered, he looked at Hawthorne over the barrel of his gun and said, "Get me a sack, Mr. Hawthorne, right quick!"

"I will not," Hawthorne said, puffing up his chest bravely.

Clem glared at him, then looked at Cora. He switched the gun so that it was pointing at her instead of the manager, and said, "Either you get me a sack, or I'm gonna shoot her!"

Hawthorne decided that it was all right to be brave with his life, but not Cora's.

"All right, all right," he said.

"And you get me a *sack*," Clem said. "You come out with a gun and I'm gonna kill both of you."

"All right, just take it easy," the portly bank manager said. "I'll get a sack."

He looked around for a few moments, then finally went into the safe to get a money sack. While in there, he grabbed the hideaway gun that he had kept in there for the past twelve years, an old Navy Colt. Hiding it behind the sack, he left the safe, determined to protect his bank's money and his employees.

"I've got the sack," he said, coming out the door. As he did so, his foot caught on the doorsill and he tripped, dropping the sack, but hanging onto the gun.

"What—" Clem Bucket said, spotting the gun.

Hawthorne was down on one knee with the gun hanging from his finger by the trigger guard and as he looked down the barrel of Clem's gun, he cried out, "No, wait—"

Clem couldn't wait, though. He fired at the bank manager, striking him in the chest. He rushed forward, grabbed the fallen sack, and then went back to the window and began stuffing it with bills.

Down the street, Marshal Dale Leighton heard the shot and rushed from his office, where he'd been having lunch. Leighton had been the law in Palmerville for six years now. He felt sure that this would be a case of another drunken cowboy shooting up the saloon, but his response was always as quick as it would have been for something more serious.

Like a bank robbery.

"It came from the bank, Marshal," someone in the street shouted.

"The bank?" Leighton said. *Impossible!*

There hadn't even been an attempted bank robbery during the six years he'd been marshal.

He looked down at the bank and sure enough, there was a man out front holding two horses, looking around nervously.

"Shit," Leighton said, drawing his gun.

As he neared the bank on the run he heard the man outside yell, "Come on, Clem," and recognized him. It was Ethan Bucket, which meant that his brother, Clem, was inside the bank.

"Ethan Bucket," he shouted. The Bucket boys had never broken any major laws in Palmerville, and Leighton was surprised to find them in a situation like this. So surprised, in fact, that he got careless.

His gun was in his right hand, but it was pointing at the ground. When Ethan Bucket turned to face him, he brought up an old .45—the mate to the one his brother Clem had used to shoot the bank manager—and he fired blindly at the marshal.

Leighton felt the shock as the bullet struck him in the upper right arm, and he felt his arm go dead and drop his gun. He fell to his knees, left hand clasped over the wound in his right arm.

"Come on," he heard Ethan shout, "I done shot the marshal!"

Using his left arm to guide his right, Leighton maneuvered his hand over the gun so he could pick it up. Once he had it, he lay down prone in the street, feeling he'd present less of a target, and he'd be able to anchor his elbow on the ground so he could shoot. He tried to block out the pain and concentrate on Ethan Bucket.

With his elbow in the dirt and his left hand holding his right wrist, he sighted on the younger Bucket and fired, just as Clem came out of the bank.

Clem watched as the bullet caught his brother in the neck, spun him around and dropped him. Enraged, he turned and saw Leighton getting up on his knees, holding his right wrist in his left hand, still. He and Leighton both fired at the same time. Leighton was hit in the left side, underneath the heart, and Clem Bucket was struck high on the left side, and fatally.

Leighton didn't see Clem Bucket fall, though, because he was already facedown in the dirt.

Leighton was carried to Doc Tillery's office, and the two Bucket brothers were taken to the morgue, along with the bank manager, Mr. Hawthorne.

Amanda Leighton, the marshal's wife, rushed to the doctor's office as soon as she heard what happened.

"Doc?" she said, entering the office. The doctor had just come out of his examining room and was talking to Leighton's deputy, Jason Handle, when she came in.

"Amanda—" the doctor said, taking her shoulders in his hands.

"How bad is he?" she asked.

"He was hit twice, Amanda. Once in the right arm, and once in the left side, just underneath his heart," he said, tapping the spot beneath his heart.

She digested the information as a lawman's wife, without histrionics, and asked, "How is he?"

"I got the bullet out of his chest," the doc said,

and she breathed easier, assuming that the chest wound was the more serious of the two.

"Then he'll be all right," she said. "He'll live."

"He'll live, Amanda," the doc said. "I can save his life, but I can't save his arm."

"What?" she asked, aghast.

"I have to take the arm to save his life," the doc explained. "The bullet did too much damage."

She stared at him with eyes that were filling with tears, then turned away, hugging herself as if she was cold.

"Amanda," the doctor said from behind, "it's up to you."

Take her husband's arm? Even if it saved his life, what would Dale say when he found out? How would he feel?

Damn it, this was his *life* they were talking about. Whatever he thought when he found out, she wanted him alive!

"Take his arm," she said, and broke into tears.

1

September 1873

Palmerville, Wyoming didn't seem like a heck of
a lot as I rode into town. There were signs that it
was growing—new buildings, new boardwalks—
but it was still a small town, and would continue to
be a small town for some time.

I stopped in front of a saloon called The Red
Bull and tied Duke off—not that I thought he
would go anywhere if I didn't, but seeing a horse
that was not tied was often an invitation to someone to try and steal it. If anyone tried to climb up
on Duke's back and steal him, the chances were
good that the thief would end up being stomped to
death anyway.

The saloon fit right in with the rest of the town—
small, but expanding. There was some construction work going on in the back, out of sight, but the
loud banging of a hammer was clearly audible.

I walked to the bar and ordered a cold beer.

"Wet I got," the bartender said, and put it
down in front of me. "but cold . . ."

"I guess I'll have to settle for wet," I said,
picking it up. I carried it to a corner table, where
I sat with my back to the wall and once again examined my motives for coming to Palmerville.

From my shirt pocket I took the folded up letter that had followed me across three states and found me in Texas, in Panhandle country.

It was from Amanda Leighton—only when I knew her, she had been Amanda Wheeler.

The letter from Amanda Wheeler Leighton had been something of a bitter pill for me to swallow. We had met in Arkansas, after I had left Stratton, Oklahoma about fourteen years ago. We had been thinking about getting married, but I was on the rebound and had taken too long to do my thinking.

Amanda up and married Dale Leighton.

Dale and I had been deputies together, but after their wedding I had chosen to move on once again—with a different attitude towards women, too. After two close calls, I had never again come close to even thinking about getting married.

The last time I had seen Dale and Amanda Leighton had been nigh onto fourteen years ago, and then I got this letter asking for my help. That was all it said: Would I come to Palmerville, Wyoming because she needed help.

She had a lot of nerve, asking me that after all of these years.

I left the Panhandle country the next day and headed for Palmerville, Wyoming.

Some of my thinking about women hadn't changed at all.

I finished my wet beer, and by that time I still hadn't changed my mind about helping Amanda out of whatever trouble she was in, so I brought the empty mug back to the bar and asked the bartender, "Where does Marshal Leighton live?"

"Marshal?" the bartender asked, shaking his head.

"Yeah, marshal," I said. "He is the marshal of this town, isn't he?"

"Yeah, I guess he still is," the bartender said. "He lives in a house at the north end of town."

"Thanks," I said, puzzled by his reaction to the question.

"Sure. Stop in again."

I left the saloon, mounted Duke and rode him towards the north end of town. I couldn't help wondering what Amanda would look like after all these years. I remembered her as a tall, stately looking young woman with long, red hair and green eyes. A full-bodied woman, I wondered if the years had cost her any weight. A lawman's wife does not live a very easy life, and I hoped she hadn't aged beyond her years.

Dale had been a little older than Amanda and I, a tall, rangy man that aging would not ever change drastically. Maybe a little gray hair here and there, but all in all Dale's kind of man looked the same at forty as he did at twenty-five.

I recognized the house by the white picket fence that surrounded it. Apparently, Dale had finally given Amanda what she had wanted all those years ago, her own home, and a white picket fence. I wondered if there was a garden out back.

I rode Duke up to the fence and left him there, untethered. I walked through the white picket gate to the house and knocked on the front door. I could hear footsteps approaching from within, and then the door swung open and there stood Amanda Wheeler Leighton.

She *had* changed. She certainly looked older than the Amanda I remembered, but she looked even lovelier than I remembered. I had been afraid that perhaps my memory of her beauty had been exaggerated by the years, but, if anything, my memory of her didn't do her justice.

"Hello, Amanda."

"Hello, Clint."

There was an awkward silence that followed our greeting, as we examined each other.

"You've changed," she said, finally breaking the silence.

"So have you," I said. "You're even more beautiful than you were as a kid."

She laughed and said, "We were more than kids, Clint."

"Not much, though," I added.

"Come in."

"Is Dale home?"

She lowered her eyes and said, "Yes. Come in, please."

She backed up and I entered, closing the door behind me.

"Come into the living room," she said, and I followed her there. She was wearing a faded dress that had seen better days, and a pair of shoes that had been repaired more than once.

The house was small and sparsely furnished with furniture that was almost as old as we were.

She turned and saw me taking in the surroundings.

"I know, we haven't done very well," she said.

"That wasn't what I was thinking at all," I insisted.

"It doesn't matter," she said, shrugging. "Can I get you a drink, Clint?"

"I don't think so. I think I'd just like to know what this is all about."

She sat down on the couch and smoothed her skirt down over her legs.

"I wasn't sure you'd come," she said.

"Well, I did," I said, not wanting to go into my reasons. "Now I'd like to know why you asked me to come. Where's Dale, anyway?"

"Dale is the reason I asked you to come," she said. "Before you see him I have to tell you something."

"What?"

"Something that happened a few months ago."

"You asked me to come here because of something that happened a couple of months ago?"

"Yes."

I sat down in a worn armchair and said, "All right, Amanda, I'm listening."

"Dale's been marshal of Palmerville for six years, Clint, and he's been a good one."

"He always was a good lawman," I said.

"And he still is," she said, and from the tone of her voice I wondered who she was trying to convince. Her remark reminded me of the one made by the bartender, and I started to wonder what was going on.

"Amanda, what's going on?" I asked.

She was about to answer when I heard footsteps from the back of the house, and a man's voice called out.

"Amanda, god damn it, you forgot to button my shirt," Dale shouted as he walked into the room.

I wasn't sure who was more surprised when we saw each other, but I think I had a slight edge.

His left hand was holding his shirt closed, but where his right arm should have been there was just an empty sleeve, dangling. With great difficulty, I pulled my eyes away from the empty sleeve and looked at his face. That shocked me even more. His face was drawn and crisscrossed with lines and creases. The man who I thought could never age looked years older than he should have. He was six foot two—he'd always been a fine figure of a man—but if he weighed a hundred and forty pounds at that moment, it was a hell of a lot.

"Clint Adams," he said, clearly showing his surprise.

"Hello, Dale," I said. I almost started towards him, but I had to stop myself, because I would have offered my right hand to shake. I also had to stop myself from automatically asking, "How are you?"

"It's good to see you, boy," he said. He walked up to me and clapped me on the right shoulder, a look of genuine pleasure in his eyes.

"Let me get your shirt, dear," Amanda said, stepping in between us.

As she buttoned his shirt for him he looked at me ruefully and said, "I guess this is sort of a shock to you, eh?"

I didn't know what to say, so I just said, "Dale . . ." and let it trail off.

"Look," he said, stepping away from Amanda, "I've got to go and practice my one-handed shaving. Why don't you let Amanda explain, okay? And plan on staying for lunch . . . and dinner. I'll see you later, all right?"

"Sure, Dale," I said.

He left the room as if he were in a hurry to get away, and truth be told I was glad when he did.

"Amanda—" I started, but she waved a hand at me for silence, and then put the hand over her mouth. I walked up to her and took her by the shoulders.

"How?" I asked. "When?"

She pressed her hand against her lips, as if trying to stifle a cry, or a scream, and then she dropped her hand and said, "A—a couple of months ago. It was—so senseless!" she hissed, trying to keep her voice down.

"All right," I said, trying to keep her calm. "Just tell me about it, okay?"

She nodded, and backed away from me. I dropped my hands to my side and waited for the explanation.

"There was a bank robbery," she said. "The first bank robbery in the six years that we've been in this town. A couple of local boys decided they wanted to leave town, and needed some money to do so. When the shooting started, Dale came running, but admittedly he was careless, and he was shot, twice."

"And the two men?"

"He killed them both, but he was nearly killed himself. The doctor was able to save his life, but . . ." and she trailed off there and covered her mouth with her hand again.

"But he had to take his arm to do it," I finished for her, and she nodded.

"Is Dale still the marshal?" I asked.

"Technically, yes."

"Does he have deputies?"

"One, Dave Morgan."

She stopped speaking and seemed to stare off into space. I didn't want to lose her, because I still didn't know why she had asked me to come, so I said, "Amanda. Amanda!"

"Yes?"

"I'll take that drink now," I said. "Whiskey."

"Oh, of course."

I sat back in the armchair and when she brought me the drink I said, "Amanda, tell me why I'm here."

She crossed the room and sat heavily on the couch.

"I didn't know what else to do," she said. "Dale has been terribly depressed since . . . since it happened. Still, he's refused to give up his badge."

"They've asked for it?" I asked.

"Yes. There's a judge coming to town in a few weeks to determine whether or not Dale is fit to go on being a United States marshal."

"And he isn't," I said.

"But he could be," she said. "You could help him."

"Me? How?"

She leaned forward now, finally getting to the point.

"Dale always said you were the best man with a gun he ever saw," she said.

"So?"

"He always said you could teach a right-handed bear how to shoot left-handed."

"Uh-huh," I said, suddenly understanding what she was getting at. "You want me to teach him to shoot with his left hand?"

"Yes, if you will," she said in a rush. It was as if she were relieved to have finally gotten to the point.

"What does Dale want?" I asked, uncomfortable with the request.

"I don't really know what he wants, Clint," she said. "I thought maybe you could talk to him."

"He didn't know you sent for me?" I asked, knowing the answer.

"Oh, no, I couldn't tell him that. You'll have to make like you just happened into town."

I scratched my head and said, "Well, I asked for him at the saloon, but I guess I could say that I'd heard he was marshal here."

"Then you'll do it!" she said.

I hadn't realized it myself, but yeah, I had pretty much decided to do it. Hell, I'd left my rig behind and ridden all the way up here, hadn't I? I wasn't about to waste the trip.

"Yeah, I'll do it," I said, "but I want you to understand something. The final decision has to be Dale's."

"You're not going to tell him—"

"I'm going to talk to him," I said. "I won't tell him it was your idea. I'll say it's mine, and we'll see how he reacts to it."

"Thank you, Clint," she said, her eyes brimming over with her gratitude. "Thank you."

"Don't thank me yet," I said, standing up and getting ready to go.

"Aren't you staying for lunch?" she asked, rising with me.

"No," I said. "I have to get settled and get my horse settled. Besides, I've got to get used to the idea of Dale . . . well, I guess he's got to get used to the idea of me being around, as well."

"I suppose so," she agreed. "You will come by for dinner, though, won't you?"

"Sure, Amanda. What time?"

"About six?"

"I'll be here," I promised.

When I left and climbed up on Duke's back, all I could think about was Dale Leighton's empty right sleeve. He had been a pretty good man with a gun, himself. Being marshal of a small, sleepy town had lulled him to sleep, and he had paid a price for it.

For me, it would have been the ultimate price, probably worse than death.

2

I put Duke up at the livery stable with the usual instructions to the man to take extra good care of him, then went and registered in the hotel.

I went up to my room only long enough to drop off my gear, then walked over to the jailhouse. I wanted to have a talk with Dale's deputy, Dave Morgan.

I knocked on the door of the small, wood-frame jailhouse and opened it when a voice invited me to.

When I walked in I saw a man of about twenty-five seated behind a desk, with his feet up.

"What can I do for you, stranger?" he asked.

I closed the door and approached the desk.

"Are you Dave Morgan?" I asked.

"Deputy U.S. Marshal Dave Morgan," he said proudly, with a touch of cockiness. "Do I know you?"

"No, you don't," I said. "I'm a friend of the Leightons."

"Is that so?" he asked. "The marshal . . . or Mrs. Leighton?"

I didn't like the tone of voice with which he asked that question, but I answered, "Both," without remarking further.

"Uh-huh. What might your name be?"

"Adams," I said, "Clint Adams."

"No shit?" he said, dropping his feet to the floor and sitting up. "Clint Adams, the Gunsmith?"

"I've been called that, yeah," I answered.

"If that don't beat all," he said, looking me up and down. "You know, I've heard stories about you."

"Don't believe everything you hear," I advised him.

"Hell," he replied, "if I only believed half of what I've heard about you, you'd still come out looking like some kind of legend."

He stood up then, and hitched his gunbelt up on his hips. He wore a .44 Remington tied down on his thigh, and I had seen his kind before enough to know what was coming next.

"You know," he said, "I fancy myself to be pretty good with a gun, myself."

"Is that so?" I asked.

"Yeah. I've always wondered how I'd stack up beside somebody like you, or Hickok."

"Don't even say my name in the same breath as Bill's," I said.

"You know Hickok?"

"We've backed each other up from time to time."

"He's real fast, ain't he?"

"He's the best, son," I said. Never having had the urge to go up against Bill and see who really was faster, I just accepted the fact that he was, and let it go at that. Bill liked his reputation, anyway, and I would rather have his reinforced than mine.

"Yeah . . ." he said, with a dreamy look in his

eyes. Another small-town would-be gunman. I hoped I wouldn't have any trouble with him while I was there. I had been hoping that Dale's deputy would turn out to be an experienced man, and not an inexperienced, gun-happy kid.

"I guess you heard about the marshal's trouble, huh?" he asked.

"That's why I'm here," I said.

"Oh, yeah?"

"To help, if I can."

"Well, I don't see how you could do that, less'n you wanna give the marshal one of your arms."

"I just thought I'd give him some moral support," I said. "You a friend of the marshal's?" I asked.

"Nope," he answered quickly. "I'm just his deputy—and maybe pretty soon I'll be the marshal."

"Really?" I asked. "Have you got the qualifications for the job?"

"I been Leighton's deputy for two years," he said, and then he dropped his hand to his gun and said, "And I told you, I'm pretty good with this here iron. Wanna see?"

"Son," I said, warningly, "don't go pulling that gun out unless you mean to use it. That's a fine way of getting yourself killed one of these days."

He narrowed his eyes and asked, "Are you threatening me?"

"Hell, no," I said. "I'm just giving you some good advice. A gun is not something to play with."

"I know that," he retorted. "I ain't no kid, you know. I'm a deputy U.S. marshal, you know."

"Yeah, I know," I answered. I could see that

I wasn't going to get the help I wanted here. This kid just couldn't wait until he became a full-fledged U.S. marshal, and by his own admission, he wasn't a particular friend of Dale Leighton's.

"Well, I guess I'll get over to the saloon and wash away some trail dust," I said.

"Was there something you wanted?" he asked.

I looked at him for a moment, then said, "No, I don't think there's anything you can help me with. I just thought I'd let you know that I was in town."

"Well, that's right neighborly of you," he commented. "Will you be in town long?"

"I hope not," I said, heading for the door. "I sincerely hope not."

3

I went to the doctor's office next, hoping I'd find more help there than I did at the jailhouse. I asked a man in the street directions, and he told me that Doc Tillery had his office on Front Street, around the corner from the saloon.

I went around to Front Street and found a door marked R.C. Tillery, M.D. I knocked and waited for an answer. The door was opened by a medium-sized man with gray hair and a gray stubble of beard. He was obviously in his mid-fifties, so the gray was well-earned.

"Doc Tillery?" I asked.

"That's me," he said. "What can I do for you?"

"Can I come in for a few minutes?"

He backed up and said, "Come ahead, son."

I walked in and he shut the door behind us, then turned to me, rubbing his hands together.

"You look healthy enough," he said.

"I don't think I've had a serious sick day in my life, Doc," I told him.

"That makes you a right fortunate man."

"I guess so."

"What is it you want to see me about?" he asked.

"Dale Leighton."

"Oh?" he said. "You a friend of the marshal?"

"As a matter of fact, I am."

"I see. Can I get you a drink?"

"No thanks."

"You don't mind if I have one, do you?"

"Help yourself."

"Thanks."

He went to a beat-up old desk and took a bottle out of one of the drawers. Without bothering to look for a glass, he took a healthy swig right from the bottle, then put the cork back and replaced the bottle in the desk.

"What do you want to talk about?" he asked, seating himself behind his desk.

"I know what Leighton's physical condition is," I said. "I'm interested in his state of mind."

"I'm afraid that's out of my field," the doc said.

"I understand that, Doc," I assured him. "I'm just asking you for your opinion."

He stared at me for a few moments, then said, "Well, my opinion would be that he's pretty depressed these days."

"Since he lost his arm."

"Yes, since he . . . lost his arm."

"Can he learn to live without that arm, Doc?"

The doc laid his right forefinger alongside of his nose and said, "I don't rightly know, son. I've known the marshal for a few years now, but I never really got to *know* him, if you see what I mean."

"And I knew him years ago," I said. "I guess

neither one of us knows what goes on inside his head these days."

"No, I guess not."

There wasn't much more to say after that. I don't know exactly what I was expecting to hear from him. I guess I was just looking for a handle on how to approach Dale.

There was something funny about the doc's attitude, but I didn't catch on just then. I guess I was too intent on one thing to notice the other.

"Okay, Doc," I said, standing up, "thanks for talking to me."

"I wish there was something else I could have told you that would help," he said. "What's Dale going to do?"

"I don't know," I said. "I really don't have any way of knowing that. Not yet, anyway."

He nodded and rubbed his hand across his mouth. I had the feeling that as soon as I left the room, he'd be at that bottle again.

At the time, I assumed it was probably guilt over having made the decision to take Leighton's arm, in exchange for his life.

I couldn't say for sure that I thought the exchange was worth it.

4

"I don't know why you had to make steak," Dale complained at dinner.

"I'm sorry," Amanda said, while she was cutting his meat and I was trying not to watch, "I guess I just didn't think—"

"No, damn it, and that seems to be becoming a habit with you," he snapped. He grabbed his fork from her and proceeded to eat awkwardly, left-handed.

Amanda looked at me with eyes that pleaded for understanding, but she was looking at the wrong guy. Personally, I thought she should have shouted right back at him and gotten it out of the way, rather than having taken his abuse, keeping her anger inside.

The evening had started out badly. As much as I felt bad for Dale, I didn't like the way he seemed to use the missing arm as an excuse to treat Amanda like dirt. It was as if he felt that she should feel guilty because she had two arms.

And then he began to glare at me, probably for the same reason. I excused it the first few times, but during dinner I was starting to get my fill of it.

Still, for Amanda's sake, I held my tongue and put up with it a little longer.

"Damn it!" he snapped angrily as he knocked his knife onto the floor.

"I'll get it," Amanda said.

"I can pick it up myself!" he said.

Amanda and I sat by awkwardly as he leaned over and picked up the knife. When he had finally retrieved it, he sat up as if to continue eating, then abruptly threw his napkin onto his plate and said, "I'm not hungry. I'm going to have a drink."

He seemed to think that whiskey might be a good replacement for his missing limb, which was why it had taken him so long to pick up the knife.

"Dale, don't you think you've had enough to drink?" Amanda asked helplessly.

"No, I don't," he answered harshly. He looked at me and said, "Finish your dinner, old buddy, and then come on into the living room and have a few drinks with me."

"I'll be in shortly," I promised.

He staggered out of the room and Amanda put her hands in her lap and stared at them.

"Don't be embarrassed, Amanda," I said.

She shrugged and said, "I don't know what to do."

"I do," I said. "I'm going to finish my delicious dinner, and then while you clean up, I'll go on into the living room and have a talk with him."

"Oh, I hope you can convince him—"

"I'm going to talk to him, Amanda," I said, interrupting her. "He'll have to convince himself, though."

"I—I understand."

"Good, now finish your dinner before it gets cold."

She smiled lamely, and then picked up her fork and proceeded to eat her dinner without much interest.

I forced myself to finish, and when my plate was empty I told her, "Leave us alone for a while, Amanda, okay?"

"I'll busy myself in the kitchen," she said.

I stood up and looked down at her, then I cupped her chin in my hand, looked into her beautiful eyes and said, "Try not to worry too much. Dale's always been a lot of man. He'll come through this all right. You'll see."

"I hope so," she said, touching my hand with hers.

I stroked her smooth cheek, then dropped my hand and started into the living room.

Dale was sitting on the worn couch with an open bottle of whiskey in his hand, resting in between his legs.

"There you are," he said loudly as I walked in. "You sure are a hell of a slow eater."

"Well, Amanda went to a lot of trouble to cook that meal," I said, "the least I could do was eat it all."

"Yeah," he said, staring at the floor morosely. "I guess I shoulda, too. I guess I ain't been treating her so good lately."

"I guess not," I agreed.

He looked up at me and said, "You noticed, huh?"

I sat in the armchair facing the couch and said, "Yeah, Dale, I noticed."

"Yeah, well, I guess you can't really blame me, though, can you?" he asked.

"Sure I can," I said.

"What?" he said, staring at me.

"It's not her fault you lost your arm, Dale," I told him. "You ought to realize that and treat her better."

"Hmph," he mumbled, "easy for you to say, you got two arms." He paused and took a swig from the half-filled bottle.

"You can't blame me for that," I said. "You can't blame anybody except the man who shot you, and he's dead."

"Yeah, I killed the son of a bitch," he said.

"That's right, you did, so now you can stop looking for other people to blame and get on with your life."

"What life?"

"You're still the marshal, aren't you?"

"Until that judge gets here and sees what kind of shape I'm in," he pointed out. He took another drink from the bottle, and now it was only one-quarter full.

"Well, if I could get you to put that bottle down, maybe we could get you into better shape."

"You gonna grow me another arm?"

"Damn it, Dale, I don't have to grow you another arm. You've already got another arm, all you've got to do is learn how to use it."

He frowned at me, then looked at his left arm as if he were just noticing it for the first time.

"You mean, learn to shoot with my left hand?" he asked.

"That's what I mean."

He sat there and thought about it for a few moments, then he put the bottle down between his feet and began flexing the fingers on his left hand.

He rubbed his hand across his mouth, then made a fist and pounded it on his knee. After that he picked up the cork from the couch cushion, and awkwardly pushed it back into the bottle.

"When do we start?" he asked.

5

What we should have done first was build up the strength in his left arm, and in fact I did start him on some exercises to do just that. Still, we didn't have enough time to wait for the exercises to take noticeable effect, so I took his Colt .45 with me to the local gun shop and borrowed the tools I needed to convert it from single-action to double-action. This would save him the trouble of having to cock before firing.

Once the work on the gun was completed, we bought a new holster from the gun shop, after a short discussion.

"There are two ways we can do this, Dale," I told him.

"What?" he asked, rubbing his fingers over his mouth. We'd been working now for three days, and he had not had a drink during that time. And he wanted one.

"You can draw from your hip," I said, "as you did right-handed, or from your belly."

"My belly?"

"Like this," I said, demonstrating. I had seen a few holsters like this over the years. Instead of hanging down along your thigh, the holster ran sideways along your belly. You would draw across your body—not quite a cross draw, however, because your hand wouldn't have to travel that far. His hand could go to his belly, and then slide the gun right out, easily.

"Which way?" I asked.

He stared at me, still wanting a drink, and still not sure that this was going to work at all.

"I don't know," he said.

"Well, then," I said, "we'll try it both ways, and see which way works the best."

On the fourth day I picked up two holsters, but only one gun belt. We practiced for a while with the conventional holster; then I slid the other one onto the belt, and he tried that way. Speed was the least of our worries at that point. Somebody had once told me, "First comes right, then comes fast," and I always believed that.

I ate dinner with them almost every night, and Dale and I discussed the day's practice. As each day passed, I began to notice something. Dale was becoming more and more proficient with his left hand, not only in shooting, but in using the hand for everyday functions, like shaving and eating.

I began to think that perhaps Dale was actually a natural left-hander, which was not odd. When people see a child using his left hand, it is not uncommon for them to try and force him to use the right hand, which is considered normal.

This might have been the case with Dale.

"Do you want me to cut your meat, dear?" Amanda asked him after we'd been working a week.

"No, thanks," he told her. "I can do it myself."

And he did, exerting enough pressure with the side of the fork to cut the meat, and doing it without awkwardness or difficulty.

After dinner I helped Amanda clear the table, and in the kitchen she said to me, "It's marvelous."

"What is?"

"His confidence is coming back," she said.

"I suppose."

"How is he doing with his gun?"

"He's hitting what he aims at," I said.

"And is he fast?"

"We haven't started working on that yet, but I don't anticipate any problem," I told her. "Amanda, I think he might even be better with his left hand than he was with his right."

"How could that be?"

I told her my theory about his possibly being naturally left-handed, and she said, "That's amazing."

"Tomorrow we'll start working on his speed and we'll see what happens," I said.

She touched my arm and said, "Clint, I don't know how to thank you."

I looked down into her eyes and said, "There's no need to."

We were still standing there like that—eyes locked, her hand on my arm—when Dale came walking in.

"Oops," he said. "Excuse me. Did I break something up?"

His tone was light, but there was something in his eyes that belied that.

"Don't be a horse's ass, Dale," I told him, moving away from Amanda.

"I was thanking him," Amanda said.

"I see," Dale said. He looked at both of us for a few seconds more, then smiled and said to me, "How about an after-dinner drink?"

"Dale—" Amanda started, but he cut her off.

"It's all right, Mandy," he told her. "It's not that I need a drink, it's just that I want one right now." He turned to look at me and said, "I think I can handle it, old buddy."

"I think so, too, Dale," I said. "A drink sounds fine."

We went into the living room, and he poured out two drinks and handed me one.

"She sent for you, didn't she, Clint?" he asked then. He had never asked me how I had come to be in town up until now, but now he'd hit the nail right on the head.

"She was worried about you," I replied.

"I can believe that," he said, sitting on the couch. I took the old armchair. "I was pretty much off my rocker there, for a while."

"If you say so," I said.

"But I'm all right, now," he said. He stared me right in the eyes and said, "I can see a lot clearer than I have in months."

It sounded as if he was referring to what he had "seen" in the kitchen a few moments ago.

"I'll be leaving, if that's what you want, Dale," I said.

"Hell, now, there's no reason for that, is there?" he asked. "Besides, we ain't finished with our lessons yet, are we?"

"No, we're not," I agreed. "We'll start working on your speed tomorrow.''

"Yeah," he said. He put his drink down on the floor and examined his left hand.

"I want to tell you something, Clint," he said, still looking at his hand, opening and closing it. "When I'm holding a gun now, it feels better than it ever did with my right hand. It feels mighty good."

"It shows," I said.

"Yeah, I guess it does," he said, picking up his drink again. He finished it off and walked back to the sideboard. For a moment, I thought he was going to pour himself another one, but instead he just put the empty glass down.

"Pour yourself another if you want it," he said. "I only wanted the one. I'm gonna go upstairs and lie down for a while. If I don't see you before you leave, I'll see you in the morning."

"Bright and early."

"Yeah," he said, "the earlier, the better. The faster you finish making a man out of me again, the better, huh?"

"Whatever you say, Dale."

"Good night, old buddy," he said.

" 'Night, Dale."

When he went up I walked to the sideboard to get myself another drink. I hadn't liked the amount of tension that had been in the air. It seemed as if Dale might be getting the idea that there was something going on between Amanda and me.

He was wrong, of course, but there was one problem: I had been starting to think along the same lines. I had been catching myself looking at her, admiring her, and sometimes I caught her looking at me the same way, both of us wondering how it would be.

Yep. The faster we got done doing what we were doing, the better it would be for all three of us.

6

"What do you mean, he's not here?" I asked Amanda. "He said he'd be ready early. Where did he go?"

I had gotten up early, as usual, to pick up Dale, but now Amanda was telling me he was gone.

"I'm not sure," she said.

"What do you think?"

She hugged her arms as if she were cold and said, "I think he went to the office."

"That's all we need," I said. "If some young gunny doesn't see a one-armed man wearing a gun and take it as a challenge, his own deputy might."

"Dave?"

"I've seen his kind before, Amanda. Dave Morgan is looking to prove himself with a gun. That sort of trouble Dale doesn't need."

"You think a one-armed man wearing a gun is a challenge?" she asked.

"I didn't realize it at first," I told her, "but yes, I do think so. Why would a one-armed man wear a gun, unless he knew how to use it?"

"Have you talked to Dale about it?"

"Not yet, but I was going to. It looks like now

he may find out for himself. I better go and find him."

"Clint," she said, grabbing hold of my arm, "take care, huh? Don't let anything happen . . . to either of you."

"Don't worry."

The town was still asleep and I walked down the empty main street towards the jailhouse. As I approached the front door, I heard raised voices from inside, and entered without knocking.

Inside I saw Dale and Deputy Morgan facing each other over the desk, with Morgan behind it—and that seemed to be what the argument was about.

"You just want to ruin my chances of being marshal, don't you?" Morgan was shouting. "You're jealous of me because I've still got two arms."

"Move out from behind my desk, Morgan," Dale said, backing away to put some space between him and the younger man, "or I'll move you out . . . feet first."

"Hold on a second," I said aloud.

They had both been so intent on each other that they hadn't heard me enter. Now Morgan looked past Dale at me and said, "You better get your friend out of here before he gets hurt, Adams."

Dale wouldn't turn around, because he didn't want to give Morgan a shot at his back.

"Get out of here, Clint."

"We had an appointment this morning," I reminded him.

"I don't need your help anymore," he said. "If you stand there quietly long enough, you'll see why."

"I'm not going to stand here and watch one of

you get killed over a desk," I said to both of them.

"There's more at stake here than a desk," Morgan told me.

"A badge isn't worth dying over, either," I said.

"*My* badge," Dale said.

"Maybe not for much longer," Morgan added.

"That's right," I said. "Next week the man who will decide that comes to town. What's the matter, Morgan, can't you wait that long? If you don't back off now, you can either end up dead, or have a lot of explaining to do about why you gunned down a one-armed man."

I saw Dale shoulder's jump when I said that, but he kept quiet and continued to concentrate on Morgan.

"Yeah, you're right," Morgan said. He relaxed, gave Dale a smug look, and moved out from behind the desk. "There's your desk, Marshal," he told Dale. "Enjoy it for what little time you've got left."

Morgan started for the door, and Dale said, "Since I'm still marshal, Morgan, I guess I've still got the authority to fire you, don't I?"

Morgan stopped and turned to face Dale again. The deputy was standing next to me now, and Dale had his back to the desk, facing us.

"Give him the badge, Morgan," I suggested. "In a week, you might have a brand new one."

Morgan hesitated, flicking his eyes from Dale to me a few times, then reached up with his left hand and removed the deputy's star from his shirt. He tossed it across the room; it skidded across the top of the desk and fell onto the floor on the other side.

"See ya, Marshal," Morgan said. He backed towards the door, opened it and walked out. I shut the door behind him, then turned to face Dale.

"What the hell do you think you're doing?" I asked him.

He didn't answer right away. He backed away from me, around his desk, and sat down, with his hand resting on the butt of his gun, which he was wearing in the conventional hip holster.

"I'm going back to work, Clint," he finally told me.

"You're not ready," I said.

"Sure I am. I've been practicing without you as well as with you, old buddy. I'm as ready as I'll ever be." He leaned forward, putting his hand on the desk and, while staring at it, he said, "Clint, I'm even faster now than I was before. It's incredible!"

I stared at him while he sat there, staring at his hand.

"I'm better than I ever was, Clint," he went on, "and I've got you to thank for it."

"Dale, I'm not sure—"

"Oh, you don't have to be sure, pal," he said, looking at me now. "*I'm* sure. I'm sure that I'm going to be able to keep my job, and I'm sure that, after today, I don't want you in my town . . . or around my wife."

I should have expected it, but I was surprised, anyway.

"Dale, you're not being fair."

"To you?" he said. "No, no, I realize that I owe you a lot, but I also realize that you only helped me because Amanda asked you to."

"You're not being fair to Amanda, Dale," I said. "That's what I meant."

"Look," he said, "don't you worry about my wife. I'll take care of her, just as I have all of these years that we've been married."

"You're saying you want me out of town," I said.

"That's right," he answered, standing up. "Leave on your own, Clint. You were better than me with a gun before, but not by that much. Now I'm better than I ever was . . . and maybe I'm even better than you. To tell you the truth, I wouldn't mind finding out," he added.

"I would."

"Sure you would. Amanda wouldn't like it if you killed me, so why don't you just leave town, huh? Don't even stop to say goodbye to her."

"Dale—"

"Get out of my town, Clint," he said. *"Now!"*

7

July 1874

I didn't hear much about Dale Leighton and Palmerville, Wyoming over the next ten months. In fact, once I got back to Texas and picked up my rig, I never really got all that close to Wyoming, to where news might have traveled.

It wasn't until I was in Lorenville, Colorado, not all that far from the border, that I even thought about Leighton again, and then it was as if I were thinking about a friend who had died.

I had been in Colorado only about a day or so, just passing through, when I met up with a girl and a poker game.

The girl came first.

Her name was Holly Bigelow and she worked in the general store. I went in there to buy some supplies, and when we saw each other it was like we'd been waiting all year for this. I'm not saying it was love at first sight or anything like that, but there was something in the air that couldn't be ignored.

"Hello," I said.

"Howdy," she replied. We were both pretty much pressed up against the counter that stood between us, and if it hadn't been there, I think we would have been pressed up against each other.

"I wonder if you could help me with a few things," I said.

"Just name them," she said.

I did. I named some bacon, coffee, canned beans and fruit, and a visit to my hotel room that night.

It was a bold move, but I was sure that she felt exactly what I was feeling.

She was a tall, dark-haired girl in her early twenties, full lipped and full bodied, with rather wide-set brown eyes and flaring nostrils. When they flared even more, I knew that her answer would be yes.

I left with my supplies, and her promise to come to my room at ten that evening.

At eight, I was playing poker in the town's only saloon, when the man seated across from me, a fellow named Dan Porter, mentioned something about just having come from Palmerville.

"That crazy lawman still there?" a second man, by the name of Will, asked. "The one with only one arm?"

"Yeah, he's still there," Porter answered.

"That guy's crazy," Will said. "Braces almost every stranger who comes to town. Tries to get them to go for their gun so he can show everyone how good he is."

I was sitting there with a full house, so I said, "I raise," but I was still listening.

The hand ended with me winning the pot, beating Dan Porter's straight.

"Did he kill anybody while you was there?" Will asked, shuffling the cards.

"No," Porter answered. "I got out of that town

real quick. He's just crazy enough to be mighty fast with that one arm."

"Oh, he's fast, all right," Will said, dealing the cards for five card stud. "I saw him gun down a young fella while I was there."

"Who?" I asked.

Will looked at me, then said, "I don't know. Just a young fella. I think somebody said that he used to be a deputy."

Dave Morgan. One of them had finally forced a facedown, and Dale had won.

"It's your bet, mister," Will said to me. I looked down and saw that he had dealt me an ace face up. I checked my hole card, and there was another ace.

"I open for ten," I said, throwing ten dollars in, annoyed at myself for having to be told that it was my bet. I don't usually play poker unless I can concentrate freely.

I had been doing all right before the talk of Palmerville and its crazy marshal.

"Somebody's gonna pull that marshal up short one of these days," Porter commented.

"Somebody should," Will said. "He's killed more men in the last six months—so I heard."

My third card was a king, and with ace, king showing, I bet twenty. Will and Porter called, and the other two players dropped out.

Will had a three and a five showing, which meant he must have had a pair. Porter had a nine and a ten.

"Yeah, the way I heard the story," Will said, "he was about washed up when he lost his arm, but somebody came in and taught him how to use that other arm of his."

"Seems to me that guy is just as responsible as the one-armed marshal for the men he's killed," Dan Porter said.

"That don't necessarily go," I said, looking at both of them.

Porter looked at me and said, "I'm just saying that's one way of looking at it."

Will dealt out our fourth cards. I caught a queen, while Will paired his threes, and Porter pulled an eight.

"Threes bet," Will said, throwing twenty into the pot. I called, and so did Porter.

"Maybe this marshal's friend just wanted to help," I suggested.

"He helped, all right," Porter said. "He helped his friend plant some people in the ground."

"He kill anyone who deserved killing, I wonder?" Will asked.

"Who knows," Porter said. "Come on, deal out that last card."

Will dealt me another ace, giving me three of them. Porter got a seven, giving him an up and down straight on the table, and Will paired his fives, giving him two pair showing.

"Dealer bets fifty," he said, throwing it in. I saw his fifty, then hit him back once for another fifty.

Porter had a good hand showing to bluff with, and that's just what he did, only he took too long to decide, and gave it away as a bluff.

Will called Porter's raise, and didn't reraise, so I knew I had the winning hand. I raised Porter back, he called, and Will folded.

I showed my third ace and Porter cursed and buried his cards.

"That's it for me, gents," I said, pulling in my winnings.

"You only played for about an hour," one of the others complained. "Give us a chance to win it back."

"Sorry," I said, "but I just lost my appetite for poker."

"Forget it," Porter told the others, "with him gone, somebody else has to win."

I went to the bar and got a bottle of whiskey to take back to my room with me. I had some thinking to do before Holly Bigelow kept our appointment.

8

"I don't usually do this, you know," she said when I'd opened the door to her knock. She was wearing a man's shirt, with the top three buttons undone, and a pair of jeans. The deep valley between her full breasts was plainly visible.

"I know," I assured her.

She walked in and I shut the door behind her.

"You felt it too, didn't you?" she asked, undoing the remaining buttons and peeling the shirt off.

"Yes, I felt it," I said. I walked up to her as she dropped the shirt to the floor, and filled my hands with her firm breasts. I felt the nipples harden to my touch, and then leaned over to take them in my mouth. I rolled one around until it became pebble hard, and then the other.

"The bed," she said. "I can't wait."

"I don't want to rush," I countered.

She undid the buttons of my fly, and then my belt. I did the same for her, and we undressed each other until we were both entirely naked. After that, we fell to the bed together.

She was in a rush, but I slowed her down. I examined her entire body with my mouth while she moaned and pleaded.

"Oh God, Clint," she breathed, as I prodded and pierced her with my tongue. She tasted clean and lemony sharp, and I used my hands to pin her down as I lapped at her.

"Oh God, what are you doing to me?" she cried out, trying to lift her hips off the bed. Suddenly her belly started to quiver, and then her whole body shook. I released her so that she could writhe about beneath me, but kept my mouth and tongue in place until she was near screaming.

"Now, please," she cried out, "now."

I climbed atop her and she reached between us to grasp my hardness and pull it towards her moist and ready portal. I pierced her and drove myself as deeply as I could, and she caught her breath and sucked at me with her muscles. She wrapped her legs around me and began moving her hips in such a way that it felt as if she were trying to force me to climax before I was ready.

I reached beneath her to cup her buttocks, and started to control the tempo of her hips, matching it to the thrust of mine.

"Oh Jesus," she was moaning, "oh God, oh yes, yes, yes . . ."

Even though I was now controlling the tempo, her muscles had an incredible pulling sensation on my cock, yanking my orgasm from me.

As I began to spew my semen into her, I let out a loud moan that mingled with her cries and she wrapped her arms and legs around me and continued to milk me until I was so empty it hurt.

"Jesus Christ, girl," I said, rolling off of her, "where did you learn to pull it out of a man like that?"

She stretched luxuriously, her large breasts flattening out against her chest, and said, "It's just something that I seem to be able to do."

"What other talents do you have?" I asked.

"I'll show you," she said.

Suddenly her head was between my legs and she was cleaning my thighs with her tongue. Her avid mouth found its way to my semi-erect cock and she took it into her mouth and sucked it to its full hardness once again, but she didn't stop there. She kept on licking, from bottom to top and back again, and then proceeded to suck on it, fondling my scrotum at the same time. I felt the familiar rush building up in my legs and reached for her, but she refused to let me free from her mouth.

I couldn't get her up from between my legs, and I couldn't hold back any longer, so I stopped fighting it and shot into her for the second time that night—hell, the second time that half hour!

She reached beneath me, cupped my buttocks and sucked on me, swallowing every drop that I could willingly give her, and then sucked out a few more.

"Christ," I said when she finally allowed me to pop free from her mouth with one last, loving swipe at the head with her tongue.

"Yum," she said, moving up beside me and snuggling up close.

"Is that the full extent of your talents?" I asked.

"I'm just taking a rest," she assured me.

"You mean there's more?" I asked, wondering if I would be able to take it.

"Well," she said, reaching down to fondle my

limp penis, "of course, that depends mostly on you."

She lowered her head and began to circle my nipples with her tongue. It was a simple thing, but no other woman had ever done it to me. With every swipe of her tongue over one of my nipples, my cock jumped. As she licked me, she began to stroke my penis with her other hand, and up I went.

"Well," she said, running her tongue around my lips, "I guess there's going to be more."

And there was, plenty more. That night that I spent with Holly Bigelow was one of the fullest nights of my life.

When I woke the next morning she was already gone, which was just as well. The women who hang around until morning, looking for happy faces, intimate "good mornings," and breakfast, are the ones who think that one night leads to a lasting relationship. Obviously, Holly was not that kind of a woman, and I was glad. I didn't want to have to give her an explanation as to why I was leaving town today.

During the night—or sometime shortly before—I had decided that it was time for me to go back to Palmerville and see what kind of damage I had done by turning Dale Leighton into a one-handed gun.

I don't believe that guilt ever really entered into it. Maybe it was just a morbid curiosity, brought about by the conversation at the poker table the evening before.

Whatever it was, though, I was heading back, right after breakfast. Since I was so close to the border, I decided to take my rig with me. My intention had been to head north, anyway, so when I finished by business in Wyoming, I could just keep on going to Montana.

Depending, of course, on what happened once I got back to Palmerville.

9

If anything, Palmerville seemed to have changed for the worse, rather than for the better. Many of the buildings I had seen under construction a year or so ago were still under construction. It looked as if the town simply decided that they didn't want to finish the improvements.

I drove my rig right to the livery where I found a different liveryman than last time I was in town. After giving him instructions on the care of my three animals—especially Duke—and my rig, which I locked, I went over to the hotel and registered.

Once I was in my room overlooking the street, I decided on what my first move should be: I had to go and see Dale.

I spilled some water from a pitcher into a basin and washed some of the trail dust off my hands and face, then went back downstairs and walked to Dale's office.

I knocked on the door, and when there was no answer, I tried it and found that it was locked. I peered in a window, but couldn't see anyone inside. With our confrontation put off—at least until

I could find him—I decided to go over to the saloon for a beer.

As I approached the batwing doors of the saloon, however, out stepped Marshal Dale Leighton. He pulled up short when he saw me, and we looked each other up and down.

He looked infinitely better than he had the last time I saw him. He had put on weight and cleaned himself up. He looked more like the Dale Leighton I used to know—all except for the missing arm.

When he saw me he put his hand on his .45 and frowned, but then I was surprised when he dropped his hand to his side and smiled.

"Clint, old buddy," he said, stepping down off the boardwalk and clapping me on the shoulder. "I was wondering how long it would take you to come back to Palmerville."

"You were?" I asked, somewhat puzzled by his reaction. He had practically kicked me out of town the last time, and now he was glad to see me?

"Yeah, I was," he said. "I wanted to apologize for the way I treated you the last time."

"Apologize?"

"Yeah, sure," he said. "Come on inside and I'll buy you a drink to prove it."

I followed him inside. We got a couple of beers and staked out a corner table.

"You know, I owe you a lot, I realize that," he said. "It wasn't right, the way I treated you, and I'm sorry."

I was more than surprised by his reaction, I was flabbergasted. I decided not to push my luck, however, by mentioning the way he had been treating Amanda, too. I figured if he had apologized to me, then maybe he had apologized to her, as well, a long time ago.

"What have you got to say?" he asked.

"What can I say?" I replied.

"Well, you can tell me that you forgive me, and that we're still friends," he said.

Before answering, I thought back, trying to decide if we had ever really been friends. We had worked together, and respected each other, but how friendly could two men be who wanted the same woman? And how friendly could they be after one of them got her?

Were we friends?

"I forgive you, Dale," I said. "I take it that means you don't want me out of town this time."

"Hell, no," he said. "Stay as long as you like."

"I went over to your office looking for you," I said. "Found the place locked up tight. I guess your deputy had gone out somewhere."

"That'd be kind of hard for him to do," he replied, "considering that I don't have a deputy."

"No deputy?" I asked. "You mean, you never replaced Dave Morgan?"

"Morgan," he said, his face taking on an expression that was very hard to read. "Did you hear about Morgan?"

"I, uh, heard something about your having to kill him," I said. "I was in Colorado, at the time."

"Yeah, I had to kill him," he said. "He didn't like it when the judge decided that I was more than fit to be a U.S. marshal. He wanted to prove that the judge was wrong. I proved that he wasn't."

He sounded very proud of himself, which I was sorry to hear. I had never known Dale Leighton to be proud of having killed someone before.

He looked like the old Dale Leighton, but he didn't think like him, that was for sure.

"You sound proud of that," I said to him.

"I am," he said. "Why shouldn't I be. I did it with this hand," he said, holding up his left hand. "How many one-armed men do you know who are better than they were with two arms?"

"Physically, you mean."

"Well, of course, physically," he said. "What did you think I meant?"

"Nothing. How is Amanda?" I asked.

"She's all right, I guess," he replied.

"What do you mean, you guess?" I asked.

"I, uh, moved into my office a while back," he said.

"You mean you moved out of the house?"

"Yeah, but it's not permanent. It's just until Amanda comes to her senses."

"What do you mean?"

"Oh, she's got this crazy idea of my giving up my job so we can move to a farm, or a ranch, or something." He laughed and said, "Can you imagine me being a farmer or a rancher, with only one arm?"

"There are a lot of things you can do with one arm that you did with two, Dale."

"Yeah, and I'm doing one," he said. "I'm still a good lawman with one arm—even better than I was before. You want another beer?"

"Sure."

"I'll get it," he said, and got up and went to the bar. I watched him, and saw no money change hands. I had never known Dale to trade on his badge. Even when we were deputies, he used to pay for everything he got. He said just because he was a lawman didn't mean that he didn't have to pay his way.

He came back, carrying two mugs in the one hand.

"My arm is stronger than ever," he said, putting both beers down on the table without spilling a drop. He sat down and said, "I'm gonna have this beer and then make my rounds. Why don't we meet for dinner later?"

"Fine with me," I said. "Dale, would you have any objections if I went to see Amanda?"

"No, of course not," he said, unconvincingly. "Why would I mind?"

"Well, last time you said—"

"Look, let's forget everything I said, last time. I was a different person, then. I couldn't cope with this," he said, indicating the empty right sleeve on his shirt. "Now I can, so let's just forget what was said last time. All right?"

"That's fine with me," I said, again.

"Great," he said. He downed his beer in a few giant gulps and then said, "Let's meet at the café at six, okay?"

"Yep. I'm going to go from here to the house, to say hello to Amanda."

He stood up and said, "Uh, sure, okay. Remember me to her, will ya?"

"Sure."

"And listen, I explained to Amanda what happened, why you left without saying good-bye," he said. "She won't blame you."

"I appreciate that."

"Sure, what are friends for, huh?" he said. "After what you did for me, I owe you a lot, Clint, and I intend to pay you back."

He slapped me on the shoulder again, and then walked out. Just as Leighton was leaving, a man entered. When he saw Dale he sidestepped quickly out of his way, and nodded a greeting. Dale ignored him.

With a look of distaste on his face, the man watched Dale leave.

"We've got to get rid of him, Asa," he said to the bartender. "Sooner or later, somebody might have to put a bullet in his back."

"Luke—" the bartender said, and I saw him jerk his head in my direction. Luke looked around at me, then hunched his shoulders, leaned on the bar, ordered a drink, and stopped talking.

Luke didn't wear a gun, and he looked like a merchant.

I wondered if he reflected the opinion of the other merchants in town, as well.

10

I finished my beer and then walked over to the house to see how Amanda was taking all of this. I don't know exactly what kind of reaction I expected to get from her when she opened the door and saw me, but what I didn't expect was no reaction at all.

With absolutely no expression on her face, she looked at me and then said, "Oh, Clint. Come in."

I walked in and she shut the door behind us and walked into the living room. If anything, the room looked even gloomier than I remembered.

"Can I get you a drink?" she asked.

"I don't want a drink. Amanda," I said, taking her by the shoulders, "are you all right?"

"Fine, I'm fine," she said.

She looked older than she had looked the last time. Her hair didn't have the same luster, her eyes had lines at the corners, and slight bags underneath. Even her proud breasts seemed to sag, although it was more due to the sag of her shoulders, as if she were carrying a great weight there.

"Amanda, tell me what happened after I left," I said.

"You mean after Dale scared you out of town so fast you couldn't even say good-bye?"

"Is that what he told you?"

"Yes."

"I left to avoid a confrontation between Dale and me, Amanda . . . over you."

"It doesn't matter," she said.

"Yes, it does," I disagreed, but I could see that to her, in her present state of mind, very little mattered.

"Tell me what happened after I left," I said again.

"What happened," she said. "What happened was that Dale began to kill people."

"Just like that?"

She sat down heavily on the worn sofa and said, "Of course not just like that. I don't think he killed anyone who didn't draw first, but the point is that he forced them into drawing first."

I could understand how Dale would be able to do that. It's not hard to make a man draw, especially a man like Dave Morgan, who wanted to draw his gun in the worse way.

"Was Dave Morgan the last?" I asked.

She looked up at me and said, "Last? Dave Morgan was the latest."

"All right, Amanda. I'm here to help, if I can," I said.

"Clint, you were here to help last time," she said. "I know I asked you to help, but that's what started all of this. I think you should just ride out. It won't take very long for Dale to try and force you to draw."

"I wouldn't draw on Dale, Amanda," I told her.

"He'd make you," she said, with conviction.

I walked over to her and put my hand on her shoulder.

"I'm going to stay and try to help, Amanda. Maybe I can get Dale to see what's happened to him. Maybe I can get him to come back to you—"

"Come back?" she asked, standing up. "Who said I want him back? I asked him to move out. I couldn't take it any more."

"All right, calm down," I said. "I'm having dinner with him later on. I'll talk to him, and then I'll come and see you again, tomorrow."

"Don't come and see me anymore, Clint," she said. "I know what Dale thought was happening last time. If you come to see me again, he's going to start thinking like that again. I don't want to be the reason you two draw on each other. I don't want to be the reason one of you gets killed."

She said all of that with the same lack of emotion she'd displayed since I entered the house. It hurt me to see a woman who had always had such fire inside react this way. The fire was out, obviously, but maybe it wasn't dead. Maybe there was something I could do to bring it back.

"I'll talk to you again, Amanda," I said. "Don't worry."

"I stopped worrying a long time ago," she said, flatly, and I believed her.

11

After I left Amanda's house, I decided it might be a good idea to have a talk with the mayor. I went back to the saloon figuring I'd have another beer and ask the bartender how I could find the mayor.

"A beer," I told the bartender.

"Here ya go," he said, putting the mug down in front of me.

"Your name's Asa, isn't it?"

"Yes, sir," he said, and I suspected that the politeness came from the fact that he had seen me sitting with Dale earlier.

"Asa, who was that fellow you were talking to earlier, when I was in here?"

"Uh, what fella was that?"

"You know," I said. "Luke."

"Oh, yeah, Luke," he said.

Asa was a fat man, barely five and a half feet tall, with a normally florid face that was becoming redder and redder by the minute. His forehead was covered with perspiration, and he pulled at the collar of his shirt.

"What are you afraid of?" I asked, perfectly

aware that I had not done anything to allay his fear.

"Uh, nothing, nothing at all, sir."

"Stop calling me sir, and relax, man," I said, grabbing my beer and spilling some of it. "All I did was ask you a simple question."

"Yes si—uh, yeah, sure."

"Okay," I said. "Answer the question."

"Uh, that was Luke White. He, uh, owns the general store down the street."

"Why did he say that the town was going to have to get rid of Marshal Leighton?"

"Uh, he said that?" he asked, nervously.

"All right," I said, banging my mug down, making him jump. "Look, Asa. I've heard some things about Marshal Leighton and I want to find out if they're true."

"Ain't you a friend of the marshal's?" he asked.

"No," I said, answering honestly. "I can't say that I am."

That surprised him.

"Have a drink, Asa, on me," I said, "and relax."

He got a glass and bottle and poured himself a shot of whiskey. After he'd polished it off I said, "Are you afraid of me or of the marshal?"

"I'll tell you something, mister," he said. "Dale Leighton would just as soon kill you as look at you."

"Is that so?"

"In the past three months I've seen him take two men out of here into the street, force them to draw, and then gun them down easy as you please." He poured himself another drink and finished that one. "He's so fast with that one arm that he don't even miss the right one."

I didn't exactly believe that, but I knew what he meant.

"They say that some gunfighter friend of his taught him how to use his left hand, and he ain't been the same man since."

"What kind of a man was he before?"

"He was a damned good lawman, hardly ever pulled his gun at all less'n it was really necessary. Losing that right arm of his sure did change him," he said, "but then he changed again, for the worse, when he learned how to use the left one."

"Okay, Asa," I said, pushing my half full beer mug away. "I want you to pass the word. Anybody planning to shoot Marshal Leighton in the back had better change his plans. You understand what I'm telling you?"

He stared at me now, probably wondering what had made me change my tune.

"Uh, yes, sir," he said. "I understand."

As an old lawman, I didn't want to see a man wearing a badge shot from behind. When you wear a badge—or when you have a reputation with a gun—being shot from behind is a distinct probability. Men who have been both—such as Hickok, and myself—have gotten into the habit of sitting in corner tables, with our backs to the wall.

I didn't want it to happen to me, and I didn't like to see it happen to anyone else.

"Now, I'm going to do what I can to help this town, so I don't want anybody taking things into their own hands, unless they're looking to face him in the street."

"Don't worry, mister," Asa answered. "Ain't nobody in this town dumb enough to do that."

"I hope not," I said. "I don't want to see anybody else die."

"Me neither," he agreed.

"Good. Now that we've agreed on that, I'd like to talk to the mayor of this town. Who is he, and where can I find him?"

Asa laughed shortly and said, "He's the man you was just asking me about."

"What?" I asked, disbelievingly. "Luke White is the mayor?"

"Yep."

12

When I walked into the general store, there he was, standing behind the counter waiting on an elderly woman. He was finished, and I approached him.

"Mr. White?"

"That's right."

"You're the mayor of Palmerville?"

"I am," he said, proudly.

He was in his late forties, a medium-sized man with a salt-and-pepper mustache and no hair on his head. I hadn't noticed that because he'd been wearing his hat in the saloon, and he still had a fringe of hair around the bald expanse.

"Take a good look at me, Mr. Mayor," I said. "You've seen me earlier today."

"Why, so I have," he said, frowning. "In the saloon."

"I'd like to talk to you about Marshal Leighton," I said.

"Leighton?" he said, his face showing his feelings for Dale. "Look, if you're a friend of his, I'm sorry about what I said—"

"Look, Mayor, I'm not walking around calling myself a friend of Leighton's. I use to know him

years ago, and I was here last year after he lost his
arm, but that doesn't mean we're friends." Being
known as a friend of Dale's would not be all that
healthy for me if I was in town for any length of
time.

"Why are you interested in him, then?"

"I don't want to see him get shot in the back,"
I said.

"Oh, mister," he said, "I wasn't serious—"

"Whether you were serious or not, there might
be someone else in town who is," I said. "Do the
rest of the townspeople feel about him the way you
do?"

"I'm afraid so. He's made our lives miserable
ever since he learned to use his gun with his left
hand." He shook his head and said, "I never
thought I'd see the day when a one-armed man
could terrify an entire town."

"Is that what he's done?" I asked, disbelievingly.

"That's the only word I know of," he said.
"He walks into any store and takes whatever he
needs without paying. Men, women, and kids step
out of his way when they see him coming . . . like
you must have seen me do today in the saloon. I
ain't afraid to say that I'm scared of the man. I'm
not looking to be called out into the street." Then,
acting more like a mayor, he asked, "What's your
name, if you don't mind my asking?"

"Clint Adams," I answered, watching him to
see if he would recognize it. He looked thoughtful
for a moment, which led me to believe that he had
heard it, but couldn't place it just then.

"Well, Mr. Adams, can I ask why you're in
town now?"

"To try and help, Mr. Mayor, and I don't want to believe that the only way of doing that is to kill Dale Leighton."

"I'm sorry about what you heard me say in the saloon, Mr. Adams," he said. "I don't want that to be the way. I was just frustrated."

"I've heard that Leighton has killed anyone who didn't draw first. Is that true?"

"It's true as far as it goes," he said. "This has always been a quiet town, Mr. Adams, and it still is. The only excitement this town sees is when Leighton decides that somebody is an undesirable, and he calls them out."

"What happened with Dave Morgan?" I asked.

"The deputy? That was probably due more to Morgan than it was to Leighton. The kid was upset because he wanted the marshal's job and didn't get it. I guess he figured he'd kill Leighton, make a name for himself, and earn the town's gratitude for getting rid of the marshal." He paused a moment, then said, "It might have worked, if he had been faster."

"No, I guess he wasn't as fast as he thought he was," I agreed. "Mr. Mayor, do me a favor. If anyone in town is thinking about backshooting Leighton, talk them out of it. Give me some time to work on him."

"Do you really think you can do anything?" he asked.

"I hope so," I said. "You see, I'm the man who taught him to use his left hand."

White's mouth fell open, and I knew that he had now placed me.

"You're Clint Adams," he said, "the one they call the Gunsmith, aren't you?"

"Yes."

"You could probably take him, couldn't you?" he asked excitedly. "I mean, if it came to that."

"It's not going to come to that, Mayor. Just make sure Leighton doesn't get shot in the back. That's your responsibility and I'm going to hold you to it. Understand?"

"Uh, yes, I understand. I'll pass the word, but I assure you, no one—"

"Just remember what I said," I said again, and walked out.

Between Asa, the bartender, and Mayor White, my message would get around, but there was bound to be one or two people in town who would still want to do it their way. They were the ones I was going to have to watch out for.

I was going to have to keep Dale alive long enough to try to talk him into a change of attitude. Maybe he'd needed to prove himself for a while after he lost the arm, and then just got turned around somehow. If I could turn him around again, maybe I could convince him to quit being a lawman and do what Amanda wanted, buy a ranch or a farm. He could always get somebody to run it for him.

Of course, at the moment the key was keeping him alive—and myself.

13

When I got to the café to meet Dale for dinner, I found him to be the only customer in the place. He had taken the largest table, right in the middle of the floor.

"There you are," he said, when I walked in. "I was starting to think you'd forgotten."

"No, I didn't forget," I said. I approached the table and said, "Dale, why don't we take a corner table?"

"Why? We've got the whole place to ourselves, we might as well take the best table in the house."

"I'd just feel more comfortable," I said.

He stared at me for a few moments, then said, "Well, since you are my guest . . ." He stood up and walked to a corner table, saying, "Is this better?"

"Much," I said.

"I suppose you'd rather sit with your back to the wall?"

"Yes," I said, and sat down.

"Coffee first?"

"Sure."

"Lisa," he called out. A young girl appeared seconds later and hurried to the table. She had long dark hair and large, heavy breasts that pushed against a low-cut peasant blouse.

"Nice knockers, huh?" he asked me. "Almost makes me wish I had two hands again." He looked at the girl and said, "Coffee," and she hurried off to get it. Her skirt showed off strong, powerful-looking calves.

"Lovely," he said. "Did you see Amanda?"

"I did."

"How is she?"

"Not good."

"She'll be ready to take me back soon, then," he said. "That is, providing I want to go back."

"But you love her, don't you?"

"I don't know," he said. "She's changed, you know."

"We all change," I said.

"I suppose," he agreed. Then he leaned forward and said, "Take you, for example."

"Me?"

"There you sit, with your back to the wall, like Hickok. You and Wild Bill," he said, shaking his head. "My buddy, Clint Adams. Only you're not Clint Adams anymore, are you?"

"What do you mean?"

"You're the Gunsmith," he said. "You've got your reputation now, don't you?"

"It's not one I wanted," I said.

"But you've got it, anyway," he said. "You were always good with a gun, Clint, but I never thought you'd be right up there with Wild Bill."

"I'm not—" I started to protest, but Lisa came back with a pot of coffee and two cups.

"Would you like your dinner now, Marshal?" she asked. She had dark skin and almost black eyes. I had thought she might be Mexican, but she spoke flawless English.

"A couple of steaks?" Dale asked me.

"Fine."

"Rustle up a couple of your mother's steak dinners, Lisa," he told her, and she nodded and left. "Her mother cooks almost as good as Lisa looks."

He drank some coffee, then said, "I guess I'm pretty close to having a reputation of my own, after all these years. At least, in Wyoming."

"Is that what you want, Dale? A reputation?"

"You know what some people are calling me?" he asked, looking at his hand. "The One-Handed Gun. Can you beat that? The One-Handed Gun."

"Dale, you don't want that reputation—" I started, but he cut me off.

"Why not?" he demanded. "You've got yours, why shouldn't I have one of my own?"

"Now you're talking like a kid, like Dave Morgan."

"Morgan's dead," he said. "He wasn't good enough to have carried a rep. I am, thanks to you."

I was about to say something when Lisa came back with two plates. I thought that was pretty quick for a couple of steaks, but when she put the plates down I saw why. The meat in Dale's plate was already cut into small pieces for him. That must have been routine with him, and she had started cooking the dinner as soon as he arrived. He must have also told her to make me a steak, assuming that I would not choose something else.

"Smells good, don't it?" he asked.

"Fine," I said.

As Lisa straightened up, I saw him put his hand on her upper thigh, beneath her skirt, and fondle her. I looked up and saw that she was looking at me, with a blank look on her face.

He patted her behind then and said, "That's all, Lisa. We'll call you if we need anything else."

She turned and left the room.

"Why is the place so empty?" I asked, after tasting the food. "This is delicious."

"Ha! It wasn't empty when I got here, but I like to eat without crowds around."

"You emptied the place out so we could eat alone?" I asked.

"Sure. I eat where I want, I get the supplies I want, I use whatever horse I want—"

"You sound like you own the town, Dale," I said.

"And why shouldn't I?" he asked. "Why shouldn't I have whatever I want in this town? Who deserves it more? I gave up my arm for it, didn't I? Can anyone else say they've done the same, or equal?"

His anger was building, but what it was directed against I wasn't sure. Angry because he had lost his arm, or because I was questioning his right to "own" the town?

"No," I said, agreeing with him, "no one has given as much as you have, Dale."

"You're damned right," he said, somewhat mollified. "Damned good cook, Maria's mother," he said, shoveling in some food.

He had justified his actions in his mind. He gave the town an arm, now it was their duty to give him whatever he wanted.

I was worried now. Was he still in shock from losing his arm? Was he just confused . . . or was he mad?

14

"You want me to be your what?" I asked.

"Deputy," Dale answered. "I want you to be my deputy. I do need one, you know."

"You've done without one for this long, haven't you?" I asked.

"Yeah, that's true, but more and more lately I've been thinking I need someone to cover my back."

"I thought this was a quiet town."

"It is," he said. "Look, do you want the job or don't you?"

"No."

"Just no?" he said. "Why not?"

"I'm finished with wearing a star, Dale," I told him.

"You've given up the law?" he asked.

"No, I've just given up being the man who enforces it," I said.

"How long?" he asked.

"About four years, now."

"You haven't put on a badge in four years?"

That wasn't exactly true, but it would have taken too long to explain why I *had* put a badge on twice in the past four years, once as a favor to Bill Hickok, and once to find the killer of a friend.

"No, I haven't."

"What have you been doing with yourself, Clint?" he asked.

"Just traveling around, trying to stay out of trouble."

"That's kind of hard for you to do, isn't it?" he asked. "I mean, with your reputation, and all."

"Yes," I admitted. "Sometimes it gets in the way."

"I've read about some of your exploits," he admitted, "before and after you quit being a lawman."

"Then you knew I quit," I said.

"Yeah, I knew," he said. "I've followed your career."

"Why?"

"Why? Because we just about started in the same place, that's why, and look where you ended up and look where I ended up."

"Yeah," I said. "You ended up with a house and a beautiful wife, and I ended up constantly sitting with my back to the wall."

"Oh, come on," he said. "It's been an exciting life, hasn't it? Admit it."

"A lot of the excitement I could have done without," I said. "A reputation is not all it's cracked up to be."

"Well, I guess I'll have to find that out for myself," he said.

"Look, Dale, it's a little late to start now, isn't it?"

"I don't think so," he said. "I've already started. I told you what they call me in this town."

"Well, since I've been here, I've heard them call you some other things, as well."

"Jealousy," he said, "pure and simple."

"They're jealous of a one-armed man?" I asked, skeptically.

"The One-Handed Gun," he said from between his teeth, glaring at me.

"I'm sorry—"

"Don't be sorry!" he shouted, slamming his fist down on the table hard enough to spill the contents of our glasses. Don't ever feel sorry for me, dammit!"

He stood up and stalked out, and once again I realized how close to the edge he was.

I just hoped he wasn't too close to pull back.

15

When Leighton went out the door, little Lisa came back into the room and looked around. The frightened look left her eyes when she saw that he was gone, but then she looked at me and became frightened again.

"Lisa," I called. "Come here, please."

I tried to make my voice as gentle as I could. She was as skittish as a newborn filly—and a lot prettier.

She approached the table tentatively.

"Yes?"

"Could I get some coffee, please?" I asked. "And would you bring another cup?"

"Another cup?" she asked, looking around.

"Yes, thanks," I said.

She went back behind the curtain, and then returned with a pot of coffee and another cup.

"Do you like coffee?" I asked.

"What?"

"Your mother's coffee," I said. "Do you like it?"

"I . . . make the coffee," she said, putting the pot down.

"Oh. Well, is it good?"

"It's delicious."

"Then sit down and have a cup with me," I invited.

"Oh, no, I can't—"

"The marshal is not coming back, Lisa, if that's what you're worried about," I assured her.

She glanced towards the door when I said his name, and then looked back at me.

"Lisa, sit down and relax. I'd like to talk to you." She hesitated and I said, "Please?"

She nodded jerkily, and sat down. I poured her a cup of coffee and she sipped it gingerly.

"You and your family own this café?" I asked.

"My mother and I," she said. "My Pa died a few years ago."

"The marshal left without paying," I said. "I apologize. I'll take care of the check."

"That's okay," she said. "The marshal never pays . . . for anything."

I had the feeling she was talking about a lot more than food.

"Lisa, what kind of a man is the marshal?"

"He's cruel," she said. She looked at me then and said, "Are you his friend?"

"No," I said, "not really. We used to be friends, years ago, but I don't approve of the things he's doing now."

"Are you here to stop him?" she asked. "To kill him?"

"Is that what you want?" I asked. "Somebody to kill him?"

"Yes," she said, with feeling. "Yes, I want someone to kill him, and I want to watch."

"Because he doesn't pay his checks?" I asked.

"No," she said, "not because of that. Because of what he does to me . . . and to my mother."

"What does he do?"

"He—" she started, then stopped and looked away before finally saying, "He makes us go to bed with him."

"Both of you?"

"Yes." She looked at me and said, "When he— he feels like it he—he comes by and takes one of us upstairs, in my mother's bed."

"I see."

"Are you going to kill him?" she asked.

"No," I said. "I'm going to try and stop him, but I'm not going to kill him."

She put her hands on my right arm, and then pulled my hand to one of her pillowy breasts and said, "I'd do anything for you, mister, if you'll just kill him."

She rubbed the back of my hand over her breast and I felt the nipple harden and grow.

"That's a very nice offer, Lisa," I said, "and I'd like it a lot, but not for this reason."

I eased my hand out of her grip, and then put my hand on her shoulder.

"I want to stop Marshal Leighton from hurting anyone else, Lisa, but I don't want to kill him. I don't think it's necessary. I think he just hasn't gotten over losing his arm yet. Don't you think that's possible?"

"I suppose," she said, glumly.

"I'll try and keep him away from you and your mother, Lisa," I said. "Let me pay for these meals, now."

"You don't have to—" she started to say.

"I like to pay my way, Lisa," I told her, putting more than enough money on the table.

"That's very generous," she said, picking up the money. "Thank you."

"You're welcome," I said, standing up. She stood up also, and I was again struck at how lovely she was, how large and well-rounded her breasts were. Her nipples pressed against her blouse, indicating that she was excited by something. I realized that I was also excited by something, and I wondered if we were both excited about the same thing.

"May I call on you while I'm in town, Lisa?" I asked.

She hesitated a moment, then said, "I think I'd like that very much . . ."

"Clint," I supplied for her. "My name is Clint Adams."

"My name is Lisa Sanchez Lancaster."

"You speak English very well," I said.

"I was born in the United States," she said. "In fact, I've never been to Mexico."

"You should go," I said. "It's a beautiful country."

"So I've heard," she replied. "My mother talks about it all the time. I'd like very much to go there, one day soon."

"Perhaps you shall," I said. I wanted to ask her how her family happened to settle so far north, but I decided that it had to have something to do with her father's name being Lancaster.

"I live upstairs," she said, so I'd know where to look for her when I wanted to call on her.

"I'll call on you soon," I promised.

"I will be waiting," she replied, and I knew then that we *were* both excited about the same thing, the prospect of being together. "And I thank you for your kindness, and your willingness to help," she added.

"It's very easy to be kind to someone as lovely as you," I told her, cupping her chin in my left hand. "I'll see you soon."

"Be careful," she said as I started for the door. "Marshal Leighton can be a very treacherous man."

"Yes," I said. "I'm beginning to realize more and more just what kind of man he's become."

16

Leaving the café, I decided that it might make some sense for me to make some friends, rather than go on making people think that I was a friend of Dale Leighton's. I have cemented a few friendships around a card table in the past, and decided to try it on for size now.

I went over the The Red Bull and found a game already going on. All of the chairs were taken at the moment, so I got myself a beer and watched the game from the bar.

There were six players and they were playing low-stakes poker. There were a couple of men there who looked like they were ranchhands. Another was wearing pearl-handled twin Colts that only a man who knew how to use them would wear. The other three players appeared to be merchants, or workers.

I had been watching the game patiently for about twenty minutes when Dale came walking in. He looked at me, smiled and nodded, and then walked over to the poker table.

"Evening, gentlemen," he said, laying his long hand on the shoulder of one of the townspeople.

The man looked up at Dale; he had been holding three kings, but he simply folded them and stood up to give the marshal his seat. Without a word, the man backed away from the table and Dale sat down.

Everyone at the table seemed to accept what happened as commonplace, except for the man with the pearl-handled Colts. Still, once the game started up again, he didn't say anything.

I watched with interest as the game progressed over the next hour as if according to plan. Everytime Dale raised, the others—except for the man with the pearlhandles—would drop out, no matter what they were holding. That meant that Dale and Pearl-Handles were virtually splitting the pots.

Pearl-Handles' confusion was mounting and I grabbed my beer and approached the table as a large pot was building.

Some signal must have passed between Dale and the other three players, because suddenly they were all in the game, and they were all building the pot.

I was standing behind Pearl-Handles and saw that he had a king-high flush in hearts. He was sitting strong, and was reraising every raise. Finally, it all had to stop somewhere, and Dale Leighton ended up with the final raise, as the others called.

"Let's see what you've got," Dale said to the others.

"We saw *you*," Pearl-Handles reminded Dale, but everyone at the table ignored him.

"I've got a pair of threes, Marshal," one of the other men said, and Pearl-Handles looked at him like he was crazy.

"That beats me," one of the others said, throwing in his cards, and Pearl-Handles' eyes popped again.

"Me too," another player said.

"How about you, stranger?" Dale asked Pearl-Handles.

"Marshal, the way I play, you've got to show your cards first, and I've got to beat them, if I can."

The room got real quiet all of a sudden and all attention focused on the poker table.

Dale sat back with a satisfied look on his face and said, "That's the way you play, is it?"

"That's the way everyone plays," the man answered. "Everywhere that I've played, that is."

"What's your name, stranger?" Dale asked.

"What does that have to do with this hand, Marshal?" the man asked.

"Nothing to do with this hand, son," Dale said, "but it does have to do with my being marshal of Palmerville, which is where we are. That means that when I ask you your name, you tell me. Got that?"

I couldn't see the stranger's face, but I saw the tension creeping into his shoulders.

"I think I understand, Marshal," he answered, finally. "My name is Percy Blue. My friends call me Pete."

"Percy?" Dale asked, chuckling. "Well, Percy, this here's Palmerville, Wyoming—"

"I know where I am, Marshal," Blue replied, cutting Dale off.

"Well, good. I could explain to you why you should show your hand first, but that would take time," Dale said. "In the interest of speeding things up, I'm going to show you mine."

Dale laid his cards down, showing a pair of aces over a pair of fives.

"Two pair, aces over," he said.

"Sorry, Marshal," Blue said, "not good enough." He laid his cards down and said, "King-high flush."

As Blue reached for the pot, Dale said, "What are you doing?"

"I'm raking in my pot," the other man answered. "I don't know why these other boys were betting with nothing in their hands, but I do know that they built me a nice big pot."

"No, you're wrong," Dale said, pushing his chair back. "They built *me* a big pot."

"What are you talking about?" Blue demanded. "I got a king-high flush to your two pair."

"I can see that," Dale said, "but what you are overlooking is the fact that, in Wyoming, a flush doesn't count in poker unless so declared before the game begins." Dale looked around the table and asked, "Did anyone so declare at the start of the game?"

The other three players all backed Leighton up, to no one's surprise but Blue's.

"This is crazy," Blue said. "What are you trying to pull?"

"I'm not trying to pull anything, son," Dale said. "You ought to learn that before you sit down to play, you've got to know all of the rules."

"The rules of poker are universal," Blue complained.

"Not in Wyoming," Dale said.

"You mean not in Palmerville," Blue said.

"What does that mean?" Dale asked, tightly.

"That you've got your own set of rules here," Blue replied. "These other boys may not mind playing by your rules, but I do. This is my pot."

"You're going to have to take it, boy," Dale said, and suddenly, in a flurry of movement, there were only the two of them left at the table. "You want to die over some money?"

"I don't intend to die," Blue said, lowering his hands until they were hovering over his guns.

"Mister, he means it," somebody warned Blue. "They call him the One-Handed Gun around here."

"I don't care what they call him, who he is, or how many arms he's got," Blue said. "He ain't cheating me out of my pot. I won it fair and square."

I was standing behind Blue, and the smart thing for me to do would have been to move out of the line of fire. It was so quiet in the room you could have heard a pin drop.

Or the hammer on my gun cock.

I didn't know whether or not Dale had heard it, but from the slight movement of Blue's shoulders, I knew Blue had.

"This is the way it's going to be, is it?" he asked. He was talking about having a gun at his back, but Dale apparently hadn't heard the hammer on my gun.

"This is the way it is, son," he said, meaning that Blue either gave up the pot, or drew on Leighton.

Blue was stubborn, but he was no fool. He eased his hands away from his guns, and stood up slowly.

"You take the pot this time, Marshal," he said, and walked out of the saloon with as much dignity as he could muster.

The tension in the room broke, and Dale leaned forward and raked in the pot. He looked at the other three men in turn, and they all moved to resume their seats, and the game.

As one of them gathered up the cards and shuffled, Dale looked around the table and said, "We seem to be short one player."

He looked over at me and said, "How about it, Clint. Looking to sit in?"

"No way, Dale," I said, starting for the door. "No way in hell."

Leighton took that as testimony to his playing ability and, laughing, he chose another player at random and told him to sit in.

17

Outside I looked around for Percy Blue and saw him stalking towards the hotel. It said something for him that he hadn't decided to wait in ambush outside The Red Bull. He was probably planning to face Dale fairly in the street the next day.

I had heard of Percy Blue. He was young, about thirty or so, and he had a reputation for being pretty good with his guns. Offhand, I couldn't decide who would have come out on top, because I'd never really seen either man in action. I was satisfied, though, that I had successfully averted the death of either man—at least for one night.

I hurried to catch up with Blue and when I was a few paces behind him, I called out to him. He turned, hands hovering over his guns, and I said, "Whoa, ease up."

"Who are you?" he demanded. "What do you want?"

"I'm the guy who cocked my gun behind you," I said.

"You!" he snapped. "You're the cowardly back-shooter—"

"I didn't shoot you in the back, Blue," I said, "and I had no intention of doing so."

"You hold a gun on a man's back for the fun of it?" he asked.

"I never drew my gun," I said. "It was still holstered when I cocked it."

He peered at my face in the darkness and said, "Who the hell are you and what's your story? You help the marshal cheat all strangers who ride into town? What kind of a place is this anyway?"

"Look, if we could go someplace and talk I think I could explain a few things to you."

"Not until you tell me who you are, friend."

"All right, look. Ease your hands away from those guns and I'll answer your questions."

"Mister, my hands are gettin' closer to my guns all the time. Let's hear your story, and your name, pronto."

"My name is Clint Adams," I said.

His hands jerked away from his guns as if they were on fire when he heard my name, and he said, "The Gunsmith?"

I made a face and said, "Yeah, the Gunsmith. Can we go somewhere and talk now?"

I could tell by the look on his face that he was annoyed with his initial reaction at hearing my name. I had to talk fast, before he figured that going for his guns was the only way to save face.

"Look, Blue, I've heard of you, and I respect your reputation, I said. "If you had gunned down a U.S. marshal, you'd be in a lot of trouble right now."

"You've got a point there," he admitted.

"Just for saving you that trouble, I deserve a few minutes of your time, don't you agree?"

"Look, I need a drink. Is there another saloon in this town where we could talk?"

"Yeah," I said, "as a matter of fact, there is *one* other saloon in this town."

"Well, let's go then," he said. "I need a drink almost as much as I need an explanation for all the craziness around here."

"I know how you feel," I said, leading the way. "Believe me."

18

We went to Palmerville's other saloon, and after we got ourselves a bottle of whiskey and two glasses, we had a small problem deciding who should sit with his back to the wall. We finally solved it by picking a table that was in a corner.

"Some life, huh?" I asked.

"I guess you'd know better than me," he said. "You been at it a little longer, you're better known."

"That gives you a chance to change," I said.

He stared at nothing at that point and said, "Maybe, maybe . . . but I don't want to discuss that. Tell me what the blazes is going on in this town."

I explained to him how I had known Dale Leighton and Amanda years ago, and how Dale had come to lose his arm. I told him the whole story without holding anything back.

"He accused you of seeing his wife and ordered you out of town?" he asked.

"That's right."

"And you backed off," he said.

"Right."

"Why? Obviously, you're not afraid of him."

"No, I'm not afraid of him," I said, "but neither did I want to kill him."

"Do you think you could have? I mean, how good *is* he with his gun now?"

"I don't know, Pete," I said, calling him that because he preferred it to "Percy," for which I couldn't blame him. "I haven't seen him in action."

"You taught him, didn't you?" he asked.

"I showed him how to shoot accurately," I said. "He worked on his draw all alone, once he realized that he must be a natural left-hander."

"I see. You've never seen him draw."

"Nope. I've got no idea how fast he is. I only know that he's faced maybe eight or ten men since I saw him last, and planted them all."

"And we don't know how good they were."

"Right."

"Well," he said, pouring the remainder of the bottle out into our glasses, "you don't want to kill him, but I don't like being cheated. I could call him out tomorrow, and we'd find out how good he is."

"I don't want that either, Pete," I said. "I'm trying to save him, damn it. I'm trying to get him to realize what he's been doing to the town, to himself—"

"And to his wife?" he asked.

"Yes, and to his wife," I agreed.

"You've still got feelings for her, don't you?" he asked.

"Maybe," I said. "And maybe I just don't want anybody to get killed."

"What do you want from me?" he asked. "You

want me to ride out and let him say he ran me out?—which is what he probably told everyone he did to you, last year."

"Would that be so bad?" I asked.

"I told you, I don't want to discuss that," he said, because there we were, talking about reputations, again.

"All right," he went on, "so what do you want from me?"

"I've passed the word that I wouldn't take it kindly if Leighton got shot in the back."

"You think somebody's planning to do that?"

"Maybe," I said, and then a new thought hit me. "Or maybe somebody is planning to hire somebody to do that."

"You still haven't told me—"

"Suppose somebody backshoots me to get to him?" I asked.

"Ah, now I see," he said. "You want me to watch your back while you watch his."

"Right."

"How do you know I'm not here to backshoot him?" he asked.

"I told you, I know your rep," I reminded him. "That's not your style."

"No, it's not," he said.

"What do you say?"

"I'll think about it overnight," he said. "Meanwhile, we might as well get another bottle of whiskey—on me."

"That's generous of you."

"Well, the way I figure it," he said, "one of us owes you a bottle of whiskey, either the marshal or me."

"Why's that?"

"Well, you saved a life tonight," he explained. "Either his or mine. One of us owes you, and I'm the only one here."

"I guess that makes sense," I said.

He got up to get the bottle, then stopped short and turned around.

"There's just one thing," he said.

"What's that?"

"I just can't help wondering which one of us you saved."

"Go get the whiskey."

19

We were staying in different hotels—Palmerville had two of those, too—and we agreed to meet for breakfast the next morning, when he would tell me what he had decided.

When I got up to my room, that special instinct that I'd developed over the years was working overtime. I heard subtle sounds behind the door of my room, telling me that someone was there. I went in with my gun still holstered, because if who-ever was inside had meant me any harm, they would have been a lot quieter.

When I turned up the lamp I saw Lisa seated in a chair by the window.

"Lisa," I said, surprised—but not too sur-prised to shut the door behind me.

"I was watching for you," she said, nodding at the window.

"I can see that," I said. "What's wrong? Why are you here?"

She stood up, dressed exactly as she had been in the café. Her big breasts pushed against the peas-ant blouse, and I could see her large nipples standing at attention.

"I came here because I like you," she said. She stood up and stood with her hands clasped in front of her, looking at the floor. "I know that's bold of me."

"No, I think it's very nice," I said. "I like you, too."

"Do you really?" she asked.

"Yes," I said. "Really."

She looked at the bed almost shyly and said, "Should we go to bed now?"

I was shocked by her forwardness.

"Lisa, how old are you?" I asked.

"Nineteen," she answered.

"You don't do this often, do you?" I asked.

She shook her head.

"Look, Lisa, I'm very flattered by this, but—"

"Don't be flattered, Clint," she said. "My reasons for being so forward are very selfish."

"All right," I said. "Why don't we sit down and you can tell me what your reasons are."

She walked over to the bed and sat down. I hesitated a moment, then pulled the chair away from the window and sat down opposite her.

"I am not a virgin," she said. "I told you about the marshal, and how he uses my mother and me."

"Yes, you did."

"He is the only man I've been to bed with," she said, "and I do not enjoy it."

"I don't blame you for that," I said. "I'm sorry."

"My mother has told me for years that a man and a woman together is supposed to be a very beautiful thing."

"Your mother's right," I said.

"I would like you to take me to bed and show me," she said then. "Show me how beautiful it is supposed to be."

I was touched by her story, and her request. I was too touched to refuse, but that wasn't the only reason. She was much too beautiful to say no to, and the heat she was causing in my groin would not allow me to anyway. I wasn't *that* noble.

I got up from the chair and sat down next to her on the bed. Her eyes were on my face the entire time, wide and innocent, and completely trusting.

As I leaned close to kiss her, her eyes followed my mouth right up until the final moment. When my lips touched hers she stiffened, but then her mouth became pliant and molded itself to mine. I put my arm around her to hold her close and she put her hands against my chest. I put my other arm around her and eased my tongue past her lips into her mouth. She began to moan and pressed her lips harder against mine. I broke the kiss and began to kiss her face and neck while I let my hand stray between us to play with her hardened nipples.

"Oh, what are you doing—" she said, but I silenced her by kissing her again.

I pulled the bottom of her blouse free from her skirt and slid my hands underneath. Her breasts were marvelously firm and smooth and I proceeded to knead them with both hands.

"Oh, God . . ." she said.

I pushed her back on the bed and told her, "Relax."

I pushed the blouse up around her neck, and then slid it off her. I dropped it to the floor and began to kiss her breasts, encircling the hard, brown nipples with my tongue, worrying them with my teeth. Her hands cupped the back of my head as I continued to work on her with my mouth. While I was doing that I was undoing her belt, and then began to work her skirt off. I continued to undress her until she was completely naked.

I went back to kissing her breasts and she said, "Oh, I feel like I'm on fire."

"You are," I said, "and so am I."

I slid down between her legs and began to kiss her thighs, working my way to that wet, warm place between them. When I started to taste her she jumped and said, "Oh, are you supposed to do that?"

"Yes," I said, "and you're supposed to like it."

I found her clitoris and began to flick at it with my tongue, and then tug it with my teeth.

"Oh, I do," she said, "I really do."

Her entire body began to tense up, and then she began to tremble. Finally, she let out a loud noise that was a cross between a cry and a long moan.

"Oh my God," she said then, "what was that? I've never felt that before."

"There's more," I assured her, "much, much more."

I stood up and began to undress as she watched me curiously. Her face was flushed and her breathing was rapid, and when I removed my pants and underclothes her eyes widened as my rigid penis popped into sight.

"Oh, it's so beautiful . . . and big!"

I got on the bed with her and again told her, "Relax."

I fondled her breasts while kissing her, and she reached between us to touch my cock. I broke the kiss so she could play with my cock and watch while she did it.

"It feels so warm and hard," she said. "It looks beautiful."

She held it in her right hand and ran her thumb around the swollen head of it. Then she began to stroke the length of it with the fingers of both hands.

"Does that feel good?" she asked.

"It feels wonderful."

"Can I—" she started to ask, but then stopped, as if she was embarrassed.

I thought I knew what she was going to say, though, so I told her, "Sure, go ahead and do what you want."

She slid down and allowed my penis to rub against her face. She closed her eyes and just continued to rub up against me for a few moments, then suddenly her tongue flicked out as if it had a life of its own.

She opened her eyes and looked up at me, I guess to check my reaction. When she didn't see shock or revulsion on my face, she stuck her tongue out and licked the head of my cock.

"Mmm," she said, licking it more avidly. She began to lick the shaft, up and down, and then returned her attention to the head, where a small bead of semen had formed. She licked at it and it disappeared, and she said, "Mmm," again.

Her next move was so sudden I think it surprised both of us. She simply opened her mouth and took me inside. When she began to suck on me I lifted my hips up off the bed. Her head began to bob as she found the proper rhythm, and I matched her rhythm with my hips.

She began to moan and suck on me harder, and I didn't think she was quite ready for what would have happened next, so I took her head in my hands and stopped her.

"Why did you stop me?" she asked, moving up next to me.

"Because I don't want it to end so soon," I said. "There's so much more."

"I want you to put it in me," she said, boldly.

"Now?"

"Please," she said, "now."

"All right."

I climbed on top of her and slid myself inside her easily. I reached beneath her to cup her buttocks and began to take her in long, smooth, easy strokes.

"Oh, my God," she said, "it's . . . it's beautiful. It feels so . . . so . . . like nothing I've ever felt."

I kissed her then, and she wrapped her arms around my neck and began moving her hips in time with mine.

"Oh, it's true," she said, against my mouth, "it's true, it is beautiful. This is the way it should be . . ."

I felt her go tense beneath me and I speeded up my strokes so that I would realize my orgasm with her. As my seed began to shoot inside of her, she shut her eyes tight and wrapped her legs around my waist, beating her heels against my buttocks.

"It's so hot," she cried. "Don't stop, please, don't ever stop," she pleaded, but the well had to run dry sometimes, and when it did she pouted and looked at me with a mixture of joy and disappointment on her face.

She wiggled her hips a bit more as I started to soften inside of her and asked eagerly, "Is there more?"

She was a healthy, eager young woman who had just been shown how beautiful sex can really be between a man and a woman when they try, and I knew I was in for a long night.

20

In the morning Lisa was still there, but I wasn't worried about her becoming a clinging female, or maybe thinking that one night made a lasting relationship. During the night she had warned me not to think that this meant she loved me. She was grateful to me, she said, and would probably like to spend some more nights with me, but she did not love me. I told her that was okay.

She was so young, so strong . . . I was lucky to be able to keep up with her—but then, experience means a lot, almost as much as youth and strength.

In the morning as we dressed, she said, "I don't know how to thank you, Clint."

"Believe me," I said, "you don't have to thank me."

"But you've given me so much," she said, "you've made me so aware of the way it should be." Her face took on a look of great determination and she added, "I will never let Marshal Leighton touch me again. Not ever!"

"I'll try and help you with that, Lisa," I said.

"I know you will." She finished dressing first and said, "I will go over to the café and start a big breakfast for you. It will be ready when you get there."

"Make it two, please," I said. "I'm meeting someone there for breakfast."

A look of pure fright came over her face and she said, "Not the marshal?"

"No, Lisa," I said gently, "not the marshal. Don't worry."

She smiled, her happy mood renewed, and said, "Two very big breakfasts."

"Right."

She waved and left, humming.

I sat back down on the bed and thought about how tired that girl had made me. "The man who gets her is going to have to sleep all day just to keep up with her all night," I told the walls.

When I thought I was strong enough I finished dressing and left to meet Pete Blue at the café. I arrived first and Lisa brought out a pot of coffee for me, still humming happily.

I did not regret what I had done with Lisa that night, but I did realize that it might have just made things more difficult for me. The next time Dale tried to get her to go to bed with him, she might just refuse. I had to find some way of keeping Dale away from her until I could bring him to his senses.

Or until I gave up on him.

I had just about gone through the entire pot of coffee when Blue showed up.

"I thought you weren't coming," I said.

"I overslept," he said. "I was on the trail all day yesterday. What's good here?"

"I've already ordered their best breakfast," I said.

"I hope it's also their biggest," he said, rubbing his hands together. "I'm starved."

As if on cue, Lisa came out balancing two plates and another pot of coffee. At the sight of Lisa, Blue seemed to forget his hunger. She had changed clothes, but was still dressed in similar fashion to the day before. She knew she had a lovely body, and she dressed to show it off, and Pete Blue was very appreciative.

"Is this good enough for you, Clint?" she asked.

I looked at my plate and saw that she had made us steak, eggs, bacon, potatoes, and fresh bread to go with the coffee.

"It looks fine to me, darlin'," Blue told her, but she kept watching me expectantly.

"Yes, Lisa, this is fine."

"Good," she said. "Call me if you need anything else."

"We will."

She looked at Pete Blue then and smiled at him.

"Oh, Lisa," I said, as something occurred to me.

"Yes?"

"Does the marshal usually have breakfast here?" I asked.

Her face fell as I mentioned him, and she said, "No, never. He usually comes in for dinner only."

"All right," I said. "Thank you."

She nodded and retreated behind the curtain to the back room.

"That is one gorgeous little lady," Blue said.

"I agree."

"She don't seem to think much of the marshal, though," he commented.

"No, I guess she doesn't."

"She seems to like you," he said. "You been making nice with the young lady?"

I stared at him and said, "Making nice?"

He shrugged and said, "It's just another way of putting it. You know, more genteel."

"Why don't you find some way to put that food into your mouth?" I asked.

"That won't be too hard," he said, and proceeded to give his full attention to the breakfast.

We were working on a third pot of coffee before I finally asked him if he had made a decision.

"Yes, I have," he said, leaning back. "It isn't everyday I get to work with the Gunsmith," he told me. "I think I'll stick around for a while. I would hate to see you get a bullet in the back because I wasn't here."

"I appreciate that," I said.

"Just tell me one thing," he said.

"What's that?"

"Do you think that one of us is going to end up going up against Leighton?"

"Jesus," I said, pouring myself some more coffee. "I hope not."

21

After breakfast, Blue said he was going to go to the saloon to wash breakfast down.

"Stay away from the larger saloon," I said. "The Red Bull. Go to the other one, The Last Place."

"You think The Red Bull Saloon is the marshal's favorite?" he asked.

"I hope so. I don't want him running into you. At least, not this soon after last night."

"I ain't gonna avoid him forever, Clint," he said. "I ain't gonna run and I ain't gonna back off if he braces me."

"I didn't think you would," I said. "Let's hope it doesn't come to that, though. Okay?"

"Okay. Where will you be?"

"I'm going to go and see Amanda Leighton again, make sure she's all right. I'll meet you at The Last Place Saloon."

"All right, but you be careful, too. From what you told me, the marshal's liable to be jealous if he sees you with his wife."

"I'll watch my step."

He nodded, and we split up.

As I was approaching Amanda's house I saw the front door open, and Dale stepped out. I ducked into a doorway as he bent his head to put his hat on. He was still fiddling with the hat as he walked past the doorway I was in, and didn't lift his head all the way up until he was past me. I waited until he turned the corner to step out into the open again.

What had Dale been doing at the house? He himself had told me that he moved out, and Amanda had said that she'd asked him to do so.

Had he spent the night there?

There was only one way to find out for sure, and that was to ask Amanda.

I walked to the house and knocked on the door.

"I thought I told you—" Amanda was saying as she opened the door, but when she saw me she stopped. "Oh, Clint."

She had changed since yesterday, probably due to Dale's visit. Some of the old fire was back in her eyes, and her posture was straighter, thrusting her proud breasts forward at me.

"Amanda, are you all right?"

"Yes, I'm fine," she said, and then quickly, "No, that's a lie. I'm not fine, Clint, not at all. Come in."

She backed away and I entered and closed the door. She was already on her way to the living room, and I followed.

"I saw Dale leaving."

"He came by earlier," she said. She laughed bitterly and said, "He wanted me to make him breakfast. Can you believe that? And then when I refused, he wanted to take me to bed."

She hugged her arms and did a slow pirouette in the center of the room.

"I almost gave in to that, Clint," she said. "I'm still a young woman, I need that . . . but I was strong. I told him to leave, that I didn't want him in my bed." She stopped turning and looked at me. "Am I wrong, Clint?"

"No, Amanda, you're not wrong," I said. I walked forward and touched her elbows.

She gazed up at me and her eyes softened.

"You used to call me Mandy, remember?"

I smiled and said, "I remember."

She touched my face and said, "Call me Mandy, Clint. Please."

"Of course, Mandy," I said.

She put both of her hands behind my neck and roughly pulled me down so she could kiss me. Her mouth was urgent, insistent on mine, and I responded. I'd forgotten, after all the years, how good her mouth tasted, how sweet her breath was. Suddenly my mouth was on her neck and we were undressing each other eagerly.

"The bedroom?" I asked.

"No," she said, "Here, on the floor."

"Mandy—" I said, and she silenced me with a deep, probing kiss.

Her breasts blossomed into my hands and I squeezed them hard. She reached for my stalk and stroked it, then fell to her knees and took me into her mouth.

I knew part of what was happening was just her need, not for me exactly, but for what we were doing. I was vain enough, however, to think that it made it better that it was with me.

Her urgent sucking brought me to an incredible hardness, even after the night I'd spent with Lisa. Lisa was a sweet, vital young woman, but Mandy was mature, experienced, and someone whom I had thought about often over the years.

The old familiarity came back quickly, and we were doing the things we used to do, touching each other the way we used to.

"Now, please," she said urgently, climbing on top of me. "Now, Clint, this way."

She was on top of me, and then suddenly, I was inside of her and she was writhing wildly, driving me deeper and deeper inside of her. The maximum penetration was achieved because my back was against the floor, and there was no give. I was as far inside of her as I could possibly go, and she was milking me, drawing me to a massive climax by the sheer manipulations of her muscles.

"Oh God," I said as I felt it building up inside of me.

"Not yet," she said, suddenly, "please, not yet."

I clamped down and tried to hold it until she was ready, but it wasn't easy. I tried thinking of other things, but all I was aware of was this sweet, wild woman driving us both to the brink of a shattering orgasm.

She was in control, and I didn't mind. She was using me to satisfy a desperate need, but I was being satisfied as well.

Her hands were planted firmly on my chest as she continued to ride me as if I were a young colt she was trying to break.

It was probably due to the night I'd spent with Lisa that I was able to hold back for so long, but finally, with a look of pure joy and ecstacy on her face, she cried out, "Now, oh now, Clint, please, let it be now . . ."

I released the control I was exerting over myself and suddenly I was exploding inside of her, filling her as I'd never filled a woman before.

She continued to bounce up and down on me as she experienced her own satisfaction, and her large, freckled breasts bounced and bobbed above my face. I watched them in fascination, even after I had ceased emptying myself into her. Her waves of pleasure seemed to go on and on, and to my surprise, I remained hard inside of her.

Finally, her movements became less frenzied and she leaned over me contentedly, staring into my face, gently rubbing her pale breasts over my mouth. Her brown nipples were still hard, and I opened my mouth to receive first one, and then the other, sucking on them in turn.

"Oh, yes . . ." she said, throwing her head back and closing her eyes as I suckled her, holding her buttocks tightly in my hands.

She pulled her breasts away from my face then and leaned over to kiss me, thrusting her tongue deep into my mouth. I released her buttocks and put one hand flat against her back and cupped her head with the other one, matching the intensity of her kiss.

Breathlessly, she broke the kiss and smiled down at me, saying, "Like old times."

"Oh, better," I said, "much better."

She rubbed her palms against my chest.

"Dale has no hair on his chest," she said. "I always loved the way the hair on your chest tickled my palms."

She continued to rub her hands over my chest with a vacant look on her face, and I began to worry about her.

"Amanda—" I said.

"Mandy," she interrupted me, "you're supposed to call me Mandy."

"Mandy, then," I said. "Mandy—"

"Would you like to do it again?" she asked, wiggling her hips.

"Mandy, I think we should talk."

The vacant look suddenly left her face, and she looked as if she had only just realized where we were, what position we were in.

"Dale still has a key," she said, climbing off of me and getting to her feet. "He could walk in at any moment."

She started to dress rapidly, and I rose and also started to dress, although I thought it unlikely that Dale would come back. He had only left minutes earlier, and he had not left on good terms.

When she was dressed Amanda actually apologized to me.

"I'm sorry, Clint," she said. "I don't know what came over me. I've never been so . . . so lustful, so out of control before. I've never—"

"Mandy," I said, stepping forward to touch her, but she flinched and backed away.

"Amanda," I said, changing my tack, "you— we—didn't do anything wrong—"

"I'm still married to Dale, Clint," she said. "I've never been unfaithful before." She looked as if she were totally puzzled. "It's just that he hasn't . . . touched me . . . in months . . ."

I wondered if she knew that Dale *had* been unfaithful, with Lisa, and with Lisa's mother.

"Amanda, do you think Dale is too far gone to change?" I asked. "To bring back to the way he was?"

"I don't know," she said, still looking puzzled. "I don't know him anymore. He's a different man."

"But is the old Dale Leighton inside?" I said. "I want to try and reach the old Dale. He used to be a good lawman, a man who served the needs of the town. Now, he has the town serving his needs, bowing to his wishes, his demands."

Amanda bore no resemblance to the woman I had just made love to, the woman who had *used* me only moments before. Once again, she was the listless woman from the previous day.

"Amanda—"

"Clint, I'm tired, all of a sudden," she said. "Could you leave, please?"

"Mandy—"

"I'm sorry," she said, turning and walking from the room, "I'm sorry. . . ." and she was gone.

I decided against going after her. She was so puzzled and confused that I actually felt a little guilty about what had happened between us, as much as I had enjoyed it. Still, it was her doing, not mine. She had made it virtually impossible for me to have refused her. After all, I was only human.

I decided to leave and find Dale, talk to him some more, see if I could spot the "old" Dale Leighton in him. I had to decide if I was simply wasting my time, digging for something that wasn't there anymore.

If so, I could simply pack up and leave . . . but

would that purge me of my guilt? I was still the one who had created what people were calling the One-Handed Gun, wasn't I? As long as he continued doing what he was doing, treating people the way he did, even killing—

I would continue to be guilty, as long as the One-Handed Gun was alive, and the old Dale Leighton was dead.

I had to try and bring him back.

22

"You missed a good card game last night," Dale told me when I found him in his office.

"Stakes were too high," I answered, and he nodded as if he knew what I meant. I wasn't prepared to back up a winning hand with my life.

"I understand you and that feller Blue had some drinks together last night."

"So?"

He shrugged.

"I just wondered if he was a new friend, or if you knew who he was all along."

"I just met him last night."

"Had you heard of him before?" he asked.

"I've heard something about him, yeah."

"Supposed to be pretty good with a gun."

"I heard that."

"Not the type that would back away from a gunfight."

"I guess not."

"I wonder why he backed out last night."

"Are you asking me?" I said.

He leaned forward in his chair and said, "No, Clint, I'm telling you. Next time, keep your hand off your gun."

"Maybe there won't be a next time, Dale," I said.

"Oh, there'll be a next time, all right," he said.

"Even if you have to push it, huh?"

"I won't have to push it," he said. "Sooner or later his kind always end up going for his gun."

"Oh, so you're going to leave it up to him then?"

"I'm going to let nature take its course," he said, "and I'd advise you to do the same." His tone of voice made it sound like he was doing more than just advising me. If he felt that way about Pete Blue, then how did he feel about me? Did he intend to "let nature take its course" as far as we were concerned, as well? Or did he already have something in mind for me?

"Dale, I think we've got to have a talk," I said.

"You're hoping to bring me to my senses, right?" he asked, a cunning look appearing on his face.

"Yeah, something like that," I admitted.

"Clint, I know you think I'm crazy," he said, "but I don't think I've ever been saner in my life."

"You haven't been acting like the Dale Leighton I knew," I said, desperately.

"The Dale Leighton you knew died long ago," he said. "This Dale Leighton"—he hit his chest with his thumb—"was born the day I lost my arm. In the past fifteen years, there have been three Dale Leightons, and this one is the one I like the best."

"I think you're alone there, Dale," I said. "You haven't been treating Amanda, or the people in this town—"

"I've been treating myself the way I think I deserve to be treated," he said, cutting me off. "If the only reason you're here is to try and change me, forget it."

I walked up to the edge of his desk and put my palms on it.

"Dale, I've become aware of a lot of grumbling going on in town," I said.

"From who?"

I waved my hand and said, "Nobody in particular, but this town is not happy about being under your thumb."

"Well, that's where they're going to stay," he said.

"Somebody in this town is bound to try and take a shot at your back," I said, firmly. "Maybe you better think about what Amanda said about a ranch, or a farm. You could always get someone to run it for you—"

"I run my own life, Clint," he said. "I don't hire somebody to do my job for me. As for somebody shooting me in the back, nobody in this town has the guts to try." He took his gun out of his holster and placed it on his desk. "This is going to keep me alive, Clint."

I stood up straight and wondered what I could possibly say to him. He picked up his gun and reholstered it, then leaned back in his chair and watched me.

"I'd like to talk to you about Lisa, the girl at the café," I said.

"What?" he asked, surprised. "What about her?"

"I've heard some talk about you and her," I said. "Is she your property?"

"You want her?" he asked me.

"Yes," I said flatly.

"You've got her," he said, magnanimously. "I can have any woman I want in this town, so you can have her. She's a little young and inexperienced. I don't have the patience to be teaching her how to be a woman, so you do it."

"Thanks," I said, wryly.

"Don't mention it. Her momma, now, there's a woman who knows what she's doing in the sack," he went on, raising his eyebrows.

"I haven't seen her mother," I said.

"She looks just like her daughter, only twenty years older, and a little bigger in the chest."

"What does Amanda think of all this?" I asked. "You can't expect her to be blind to all of it."

"Amanda," he said. "She's the one who asked me to leave, so it's her doing, not mine."

"Maybe you should make an effort to—"

"Clint," he said, cutting me off, "you're my buddy, my old buddy, but don't be telling me how to run my life, or my wife. That's pushing friendship just a little."

I pretended to be a little insulted.

"Well, excuse me," I said, coldly.

"Now, don't get all het up. Friends speak their minds sometimes, that's allowed. You just got to know when to stop. Right?"

"Whatever you say, Marshal."

"Look, go over to the saloon and have a couple of drinks on me. Tell the bartender to put it on my, uh, tab."

What tab, I thought, but I said, "Sure. I'll do that."

"The Red Bull Saloon," he said. "Bartender's

name is Asa. Tell him I sent you over."

"Sure, Dale. See you later."

"Look, Clint," he said as I turned to leave. "I appreciate your wanting to help, but I'm fine. I've never been better. Really."

The shame of it was, he really believed that.

23

Instead of going to The Red Bull, I started for The Last Place Saloon. The Red Bull was on the main street, but The Last Place was on a smaller side street, and as I turned into it, I found it odd that someone would be entering town using that street, instead of the main street.

There were three of them, all wearing tied-down Colts, and I didn't like the look of them. Hardcases, all, and I figured the only reason they'd be coming into town that way would be to avoid any unwanted attention.

I started to think about what Dale had said about no one in town having the guts to backshoot him. Maybe someone had hired outside help to take care of Dale, and maybe this was it.

The three riders stopped in front of The Last Place Saloon, and two of them dismounted and handed the third man the reins of their horses. He turned and started for the livery with their horses in tow, and they went into the saloon.

I figured the two would wait for the one to re-join them, so I followed him to the livery.

Duke was in the livery, along with my rig, and I

had neglected them up until then, so I decided to take the opportunity to check on them, and maybe I'd find out something while I was at it.

When I reached the stable the livery man and the stranger were absorbed in conversation over rates, so I walked past them to Duke's stall.

"How you doing, big boy?" I asked. He nuzzled my hand while I patted his nose and strained my ears to hear the conversation going on behind me.

"Just got into town, huh?" the livery man said.

"Uh," the man answered, if you can call that an answer.

"Gonna be stayin' long?"

"Dunno," the stranger said.

"Got business?"

"You ask too many questions, friend," the stranger said then. "That can be a mighty unhealthy habit to get into."

"Geez, Mister, I wuz just makin' conversation," the livery man complained.

"You want conversation, talk to the horses," the stranger advised him.

"Sure."

The stranger turned and walked away then, and I stepped out from Duke's stall.

"Might unfriendly fella," I commented.

"You don't know the half of it," the livery man answered. "He's got eyes like steel. Like to chilled my bones, that one did. He's not only unfriendly, he's downright mean. I wouldn't want to be the reason he's in town."

"No, I guess that'd be unhealthy," I said.

"You satisfied with the way I'm treatin' yore animal?" he asked me.

"He looks fine," I said.

"Ain't never had a better looking animal in my stable," he told me. "Look at these three," he said, indicating the three animals the stranger had just left.

I looked at them. They had been ridden long and hard and needed a lot of rest and food.

"Man who treats an animal like this don't deserve to have one," I said.

"Yeah," he agreed, "but *you* tell him that, not me."

He walked the three animals to the back, where he had some empty stalls, and I noticed that the brands on the three of them were all different.

I'd learned very little from my visit to the livery. I headed back to The Last Place, hoping to find out a lot more.

24

When I walked into the saloon, the three strangers were lined up at the bar. None of them moved their heads, but I was acutely aware of being watched through the mirror behind the bar. I located Pete Blue, sitting with his back to one wall at the same corner table we'd occupied before, and I went over and sat with my back to the other wall. He had a bottle of whiskey on the table, a full glass, and one empty glass.

I filled the empty and said, "Know them?"

"The one on the left," he said. "Notice anything unusual about him?"

I watched him, and as he drank his whiskey, I noticed what Blue was talking about. On his gun hand he wore a black glove, and now I knew who he was.

"Nelson Boyd," I said.

"That black glove on his gunhand is his trademark," Blue said, nodding.

"Ever seen him in action?" I asked.

"No, but I've heard he's good."

"One of the best."

"Aren't we all," Blue commented, and he was

right. Everybody with a rep was "one of the best." The big question was, who was *the* best?

I watched Nels Boyd. He used his left hand to lift his drink to his mouth, and his black-gloved right hand always hung down by his gun.

"Know the other two?" I asked.

"No," he said, "but if they're with Boyd, they're bad news."

I nodded and poured myself another drink.

"Think they're here for Leighton?" he asked.

"Well, they sure didn't want a lot of people to see them riding into town," I said.

"One of your potential backshooters decided to dig into his pockets, instead," he suggested.

"Maybe," I said.

"If Leighton hears that Boyd is in town, he's gonna brace him," Pete said.

"I know."

"Maybe we should just stand back and let him." he said. "Might solve everybody's problem."

I made a face and drank some of my whiskey.

"Clint, you can't be nursemaidin' the man forever," he said. "You're letting your guilt get the better of you."

"Maybe," I said, thinking of Amanda. Did she still care what happened to Dale? How would she react if he was killed—and if I let it happen?

But Pete was right about something. I couldn't be watching over Dale forever. If he chose to brace Boyd and his friends, should I just stand by and watch?

Could I? If I was in a strange town, and saw a strange lawman facing three men, would I just stand by and watch?

The answer to that was no. I'd step in and help

any man with a badge, if he needed it. Dale had no deputy, so if he chose to face these three men, he'd sure as shit need help, and I'd give it to him.

If, however, he was facing Boyd alone, that would be a different story. In that case, I'd have to stand by and let the man do his job, no matter what the consequences.

I said as much to Pete, and he nodded and said, "Makes sense. I guess we'll just have to wait and see what happens."

The three men at the bar finished their drinks and Nels Boyd asked the bartender, "Where's the smallest hotel in town?"

"There's only two," the bartender answered, "but you want the one just down this street. Ain't got no name, we just call it the little hotel."

Both Pete and I were staying at the hotel on the main street.

"Much obliged," Boyd said and dropped a couple of pieces of silver on top of the bar.

He and his friends turned to leave, and as they did their eyes collectively fell on Pete Blue and me sitting in the corner. We all exchanged glances for a few frozen seconds, and then Boyd started for the door and his two friends followed.

When they were gone Pete leaned over and poured us each a last drink from the bottle.

"Ugly customers," he said.

"Yeah," I agreed.

"What now?"

"Well, friend," I said, "I think one of us is going to have to move."

"From this table?" he asked, hopefully.

"From our hotel," I said.

"That's what I was afraid you meant," he said.

"Which one?"

"We'll flip a coin," I said, and fished one out of my pocket. "Call it," I told him.

"Heads."

I flipped it up and we both watched as it turned over and over on its way up, and then as it started to come back down.

I caught it in my right hand, slapped it down on the back of my left hand, and let us both see it.

"Damn!" he snapped.

25

While Pete went to check out of our hotel, I went to the other one to buy some information from the desk clerk.

"I'd like to look at your register," I said.

"What for?" the clerk asked. He was a little weasel of a man with thinning gray hair and no chin.

I showed him a dollar piece and said, "Because I asked nicely."

"I don't know—" he said, eyeing the dollar but wondering if he could get more.

"Of course," I said, "next time I might not ask so nicely.

He grabbed the dollar, turned the register around and said, "Help yourself."

"Thank you."

Nels Boyd might have tried to avoid attention while riding in, but he wasn't hiding who he was. He'd signed as "Nelson W. Boyd." The other two names were Mike Sideman and Nick Able. Their names were familiar to me. They were minor gunmen, not on a par with Nelson Boyd or Pete Blue. Obviously, they were simply back-up firepower, just in case they were needed.

I didn't think Nels Boyd would need them to face a one-handed lawman. I hoped that Boyd felt the same way.

I heard something behind me and turned to find Pete Blue carrying his gear.

"What happened?" I asked. "Get evicted?"

"I'm looking for something a little cozier," he said, dropping his stuff on the floor in front of the counter.

"Give my son something with a view," I told the clerk.

"Sign in, please," the clerk said, giving the register to Pete.

"Recognize these other names?" Pete asked me.

"I should," I said, "I paid a dollar to be able to read them."

"That was silly," he said. "I just read them for nothing." He turned the book around and gave it back to the clerk, who gave me a pitying glance, as if he'd just put something over on me. The truth was I had put it over on myself.

"Let's go to your suite," I told Pete, giving the clerk a look that sent him searching for somewhere else to direct his eyes.

I picked up Pete's rifle while he grabbed his saddlebags and bedroll and followed him up the stairs. There was no problem about getting a room on the same floor with the three gunmen, since the hotel only had one floor of rooms.

When we got inside Pete's room he put his stuff on the bed and said, "The clerk must think it's Christmas, getting four new guests in one day."

"Only two rooms, though," I pointed out.

"Boyd and his friends took the same room."

"Which one?" he asked. "I didn't notice."

"Room Ten," I said. Pete's was Room Two, so they were at opposite ends of the hall.

"I think you had better just watch Boyd," I told Pete. "If the others leave the building, but he stays, then you stay. If anyone braces Leighton, it will be him."

"Okay."

"In the event they should end up facing each other in the street, you take Able and I'll take Sideman. We'll make sure they keep out of the action."

"Right."

"You can pull out anytime you want to, Pete," I told him, giving him an out.

"Nah," he said, "not when it's just getting interesting."

"Okay," I said, nodding. "I'll let you get settled into your new room."

"Where are you off to?"

"I want to meet Lisa Lancaster's mother."

He grinned and said, "Gonna ask for Lisa's hand?"

I waved him off and left. Asking for her hand would have been a little silly, considering the other parts of her I'd already had.

26

I went to the café, which was pretty busy at this time of the day, serving lunch. Lisa was waiting on tables, as well as another girl who was considerably plainer and thinner.

When she saw me Lisa smiled and came towards me, brushing her hair from her eyes with the back of her hand.

"Clint, hello," she said. "Would you like lunch?"

"Not right now, Lisa, thanks," I said. "I really came to talk to your mother."

"My mother?"

"Yes. Is she in the back?"

"Why, yes, but she is very busy right now—"

"I won't keep her long," I promised. "I would just like to meet her."

She thought a moment, studying my face, and then said, "All right. She's in the back, cooking. Her name is Lupe. You can go back and tell her who you are. I've already told her about you."

"Does she speak English?" I asked.

"Yes, but speak slowly."

"Thanks."

Somebody called out to her, and with a last glance at me, she hurried to see to her customers.

I walked to the back of the room, pushed the curtain aside, and entered the kitchen.

The woman at the stove was obviously Lisa's mother. She turned as I entered, and that was easy to see. She had the same features, though hers were more mature, the same full breasts, and the same powerful legs. Yet there was something else about her that stood out. Lisa was a lovely creature, but there was a sensual quality about her mother that reached out and grabbed you by the throat.

It was very hot back there, and she was wearing a peasant blouse similar to Lisa's. She was sweating heavily, and the blouse was plastered to her breasts, revealing them as if she were naked. Her nipples were incredibly large, even larger than her daughter's.

Her jaw was heavier than Lisa's, her lower lip fuller, lusher. Her eyes were shaped the same, but there was a sleepy sensuousness that the girl's didn't possess.

No wonder Dale was so willing to let me "have" Lisa. As lovely as she was, she took second place to her mother. Oh, she was more beautiful than her mother, but she was not nearly as sexy, as potent as the older woman was.

"I can help you?" she asked in accented English.

"My name is Clint Adams," I said, after clearing my throat of the catch she had put there.

"Ah, you are my Lisa's friend," she said. "Her *amigo.*"

"Yes," I said, taking a few more steps to close

the distance between us, "and I would also like to be your *amigo,* Lupe Sanchez."

She smiled, showing clean, white teeth. I was glad she did not favor the gold teeth that many Mexican women her age did.

"Bueno," she said, "You are my *amigo.* She says you wish to help us."

"That is true," I said. "I have arranged with the marshal—" I started, but then realized that I was speaking too fast for her. "I have spoken to the marshal," I said, more slowly, "and he will no longer bother your daughter."

She clapped her hands together and said, *"Aye, gracias, señor."*

"I don't know if I can keep him away from you, though, Señora Sanchez."

"Por favor," she said, touching my arm, "you must call me Lupe."

"Very well, Lupe."

The touch of her hand on my arm, as well as the nearness of her body, was tightening my groin. Even though Lisa and a lot of other people were in the other room, I wanted to strip her mother and take her right there on the floor.

And I think she knew it.

"Do not worry about me, Señor Adams," she said. "I can take care of myself with men."

"Yes," I said, "I believe you can, Lupe. And please, call me Clint."

"Yes," she said. "Cleent."

Her dark hair was matted with perspiration and sticking to her forehead, and there were beads of sweat running down her face, but right at that moment she was the sexiest woman I had ever seen.

"You are very beautiful, Lupe," I said.

"Gracias, Cleent," she said. "You are also very beautiful."

We understood each other, and I felt sure that it would happen, if not right in that kitchen, then someplace else.

Another place, another time.

"I have to go," I said.

"Sí. You will come back, no?"

"I will come back yes," I said. "Definitely, yes."

I backed away from her, not wanting to take my eyes off of her until the very last moment. Finally, I reached the curtained doorway, turned and left the kitchen.

The air in the other room was considerably cooler, but the heat in my groin did not diminish at all.

Lisa saw me and came over to me, a knowing look on her face—a look that was much older than she was.

"You were impressed with my mother," she said.

"Very impressed," I said, honestly.

"Did you talk to the marshal?" she asked.

"Yes," I said. "He won't be bothering you."

She closed her eyes, then opened them and said, "Thank you, Clint. May I come to your room tonight to thank you properly?"

"You can come to my room, Lisa, but not to thank me," I said. "You come only because you want to."

She smiled and said, "All right." Someone called out to her and she turned, then turned back to me. "I have to go." She touched my arm and said, "I'll see you later tonight."

"All right," I said.

She went to once again take care of her customers, and I left the café, still somewhat under her mother's spell.

Outside I took several deep breaths, trying to shake the effects of the meeting with Lupe Sanchez. I had never bedded both a mother and a daughter before but at that moment I was sure that, in this case, it was inevitable.

27

Taking a walk to clear my head, I found myself in the vicinity of Mayor Luke White's general store, and decided to drop in. I wanted to see how he would react to my news that Nelson Boyd had ridden into town with two friends.

White was alone in the store as I entered, and as I approached the counter he said, "I passed your message around town, Mr. Adams. I'm sure no one will be trying anything silly."

"Somebody may already have done something silly, Mayor," I said.

"I don't know what you mean," he said.

"Do you know of a man named Nelson Boyd?" I asked.

"I don't believe I do," he said.

"He's a hired gunman," I said, "and he's just ridden into town."

"I see," White said. "You think he's here because of Marshal Leighton, and that someone hired him."

"It's a possibility," I said. "He also brought along two friends who also make their living with their guns." I looked hard at him and said, "If I find out that you—"

"I swear, Adams, I know nothing about this," he said. "I'll look into it and see if I can find out anything."

"You do that," I said. "If you find out who is paying Boyd, tell him to call him off."

"I will," he said. "You can count on me."

I pointed my finger at him and said, "If I end up facing Boyd, White, the man who hired him is going to be very sorry. You can count on that."

"I swear—" White started to say, but I walked out without letting him finish. I hadn't liked the man since I heard his remark in the saloon. He hadn't fooled me by claiming that he didn't mean it. No one should talk about backshooting another man, whether he means it or not. That had to be the most obscene way to die that there was, to be shot in the back by a coward.

28

The remainder of that day passed uneventfully. As if by some silent agreement, Dale stayed in his office most of the day, and Boyd and his friends stayed in their hotel. Only Sideman came out, and that was to get whiskey and food, which he brought back to the room.

I went up and relieved Pete Blue long enough for him to get some dinner and bring it back to his room. After that, I spent some time in The Red Bull Saloon, but Dale never showed up. I got into a small stakes poker game, determined to get up and abandon the game if Dale showed up to play. He didn't, so I made a few dollars and passed a few hours playing cards.

After that, satisfied that nothing was going to happen that night, I headed back to my hotel. I wanted to be up very early the next day, so that there wouldn't be any chance that I might miss something.

Up in my room I stripped down to nothing and used a rag and the water basin to clean myself. That done, I pulled my britches back on and settled into the chair by the window.

I was thinking about Lupe Sanchez.

I should have been thinking about Dale Leighton, or Amanda, or even the risk I myself was taking by staying in this town, but instead I was thinking about how Lupe looked in that stifling heat, and the way her breasts looked through the sheer, damp blouse. I realized that since meeting her five minutes didn't go by that I didn't think about her.

I wasn't much for smoking—except for an occasional cigar—but right then I wished I had a cigarette, or the makings.

I hauled my gun out of my holster and, taking the necessary items from my saddlebags, set about to cleaning it. After that I took the little Colt .22 New Line out and cleaned that, too. The Colt was a belly gun that I sometimes carried tucked into my belt on the inside of my shirt. I had taken it off a dead man about two years ago, and it had immediately saved my life. I decided that starting tomorrow, I'd start carrying the New Line as well as my regular gun.

There were too many men in town who made their livings with their guns. I hadn't seen so many gunmen in one place since Abilene, when I was there with Hickok, and Wes Hardin, Ben Thompson, and the James boys were also in town.

I hoped Palmerville wouldn't end the way Abilene had.

I was about to get dressed and go out for a bottle of whiskey when there was a knock on the door. I remembered that Lisa had asked if she could come to my room tonight. I'd forgotten it until the knock on the door.

I opened the door, expecting Lisa, and wishing for Lupe. What I got was Dale Leighton, holding a bottle of whiskey.

"Thirsty?" he asked, handing me the bottle.

"You working for room service now?" I asked.

"Nope," he said, "I just thought I'd come up and share a nightcap with my old buddy."

"Is that so?"

"You gonna ask me in?" he asked, peering past me into the room. "Or do you have some companionship already?"

"Not yet," I admitted, stepping back to allow him to enter.

"But you're expecting someone, huh?" he said, sliding past me.

"That's right."

"I won't be long," he promised, as I closed the door. "One drink and then I'll be gone and you can keep the bottle."

"Much obliged."

"Got glasses?"

I shook my head.

"Well then, just pass the bottle over," he said. He walked to the window where I'd been sitting and peered out, then turned to accept the bottle.

"To what do I owe this pleasure, Dale?" I asked.

He spotted the .22 New Line lying on the bed and picked it up. Examining it, he said, "I hear we got some more visitors in town today."

"Oh? Who?"

"Fella named Nelson Boyd," he said. Holding up the New Line he said, "Nice gun." He put it back on the bed and picked up the bottle again.

"You know Boyd?"

"I know of him," I said. "What's he doing in town?"

"I don't know, but I aim to find out . . . tomorrow. He's got some friends with him, though, which is why I really came to talk to you."

"You want me to back your play?"

"Well, I don't have a deputy, you'll remember," he said.

"No, you don't, and I'm still not putting a badge on," I said, "but I guess I could arrange to be around."

"That's all I ask, Clint," he said, handing me the bottle.

"Dale, why brace him?"

"I can't let a man like that come into my town *without* bracing him," he said. "I'm gonna stop him right in the street tomorrow and find out why he's here."

"The street," I said. "That's an open invitation for trouble."

"I ain't afraid of trouble, Clint," he said, touching his gun. "Not while I got this." He patted my shoulder and said, "You enjoy that whiskey, and the rest of the night." He winked at me and then walked to the door.

"I'll see you early tomorrow," he said. "I knew I could count on you, even without a badge."

He left, and I was standing there with the whiskey bottle in my hand. I tilted it up and took a couple of healthy swallows, then set it down on the night table. I moved to the window and watched Dale walk across the street to his office.

It figured that as soon as he found out that Boyd

was here in town, he'd plan to face him down in the street. He must have thought—as I did—that he was the reason Nelson Boyd was in Palmerville, and he'd decided to press their meeting right out in the open, where everyone would see it—including whoever had hired Boyd.

I had a feeling that it meant something, his coming to me for help, but I didn't know exactly what to make of it. The man who was now Dale Leighton was totally foreign to me. I couldn't begin to guess what was going through his head, and I decided not to try.

I had another drink and realized that I was hoping Lisa would not show up to "thank" me. I was thinking too much about her mother to perform properly with her, as lovely and desirable as she was. If she did show up, I'd have to find some gentle way of turning her away.

At that point there was a knock on the door and I put down the bottle and went to let Lisa in.

When I opened the door, Lupe Sanchez smiled at me and said, "Lisa could not come. Do you mind?"

29

"Come in, please," I said, finding my voice after a moment. I was surprised to see Lupe there, excited, and—to my annoyance—more than a little nervous.

She entered, and then turned to face me, asking, "I did not misunderstand, did I?"

"No, Lupe," I told her, "you did not misunderstand at all."

I approached her, took her in my arms, and our lips met in a searing, dizzying kiss. Her tongue was alive in my mouth and her hands were alive on my body.

First the daughter, I was thinking, and now the mother, and that thought was making me even more excited.

She broke the kiss, but her hands remained active as she stared up at me and said, "Do not worry about Lisa. She knows I am here."

"She doesn't mind?" I asked.

"Lisa is a wonderful girl," she said. "I am very grateful to you for showing her that, between a man and a woman, it is as I have said for many years. Now, I have come to see for myself what a wonderful lover you are.''

She stepped back and disrobed, slowly, tantalizingly, knowing that I was trapped by the sight of her.

Her breasts were beautiful. She was nearly forty, but as large and heavy as her breasts were, there was very little sag to them. When she removed her skirt I saw that her belly was probably not as flat as it had once been, but the slight rise there, just above the dark triangle of hair, only served to make me want to sink my teeth into the soft flesh.

"Now you," she said, when she was totally naked. "Undress for me, slowly."

A woman had never asked that of me before, and to tell the truth, I felt a little awkward after having watched her graceful performance. Normally, I make a habit of getting my clothes off as quickly as I can, but this night, for her, I did it slowly, and I could tell she appreciated it. When my swollen cock came into view, a hungry look appeared in her eyes, and she came forward to take me in both of her hands, cradling my cock as if it were some valuable jewel. One hand held me tightly as the other dipped down and cupped my balls. Slowly, she began to lick my balls, sliding them in and out of her mouth as gently as she could, knowing how sensitive they were. Her lips then met the base of my penis and began to work their way up.

"You are truly beautiful," she said reverently, licking the length of my cock lasciviously. I cupped her head in my hands and her mouth engulfed me, taking as much of me inside as she could. It was a marvelous sensation to have a woman work on your manhood with her mouth, her tongue, her teeth, as well as her hands and, finally, her pussy.

It was warm in the room, and we both were covered now by a slight sheen of sweat. The odor of her perspiration rose to my nostrils, and it was not at all unpleasant.

Her cheeks hollowed out as she began to suck on me, threatening to empty me right there and then.

"Lupe, please . . ." I said, tugging at her head to gently disengage myself.

"You do not like this?" she asked, looking up at me, puzzled.

"I love it," I said. "You are gentle and loving, but I want to do these things to you now."

"A woman should give pleasure to a man, no?" she asked.

I raised her to her feet and moved her back towards the bed, telling her, "But a man should also give pleasure to a woman. Both should give as well as take."

"Yes," she said, and I pushed her down onto her back. She closed her eyes and moaned aloud as I began to run my tongue over her large, incredible breasts. They were firm and tasted salty from her sweat. I sucked the nipples into my mouth and continued to suck on them until she began to mutter in Spanish, rolling her head from side to side.

I worked my way down her body until I reached that soft roll of flesh around her belly, and I did sink my teeth into it, gently, as I had wanted to when she first undressed. She put her hands behind my head and, with gentle insistence, began to push my face further down. With my nose inches from her moist portal, I could feel the heat of her on my face, and smell the musky scent of her sex.

Slowly, I ran my tongue along the entire length of her moist slit, and then I parted her nether lips and slid my tongue as deeply inside of her as I could. Her belly tensed and she lifted her hips off the bed while holding the back of my head tightly. I ran my tongue around her again and again while she bucked beneath me, and finally I found her stiff little nub and began to roll *it* about it my mouth.

"Dios, dios . . ." she was murmuring, lifting her hips high off the bed to meet the pressure of my tongue and lips. I sucked on her until her body was wracked by the tremors of her pleasure, tremors which seemed to go on and on.

Finally, I couldn't hold back any longer. I raised myself above her, touching the head of my penis to her moist slit, and then I began to push into her, inch by inch into her steaming cauldron of love, until I was belly to belly with her, embedded totally in the heat of her.

"Madre de dios," she said, and wrapped her powerful legs around my waist. She covered my mouth with hers and thrust her tongue against mine as we found a tempo that suited us both and began to thrust at each other, seeking the ultimate pleasure that a man and a woman can find in each other.

I cupped her plump behind in my hands, pulling her tightly to me, and I could feel her sucking at me, milking me, yanking on me . . . "Please," she murmured against my lips, "fill me with your seed, fill me with your love . . ."

I felt her belly trembling beneath me and knew that it was time. I speeded up our tempo and suddenly I was erupting inside of her, filling her up.

The feel of her breasts against my chest, the smell of her in my nostrils, seemed to serve to keep me pumping and pumping, as if it were all bubbling up from a bottomless pit . . .

"It does not end," she said in my ear, "it seems never to end . . ."

I didn't know quite what she was referring to, whether it was her pleasure, mine, or both, but she was right. Her orgasm came in waves and that seemed to urge me on. Though I had stopped shooting inside of her now, my erection had not seemed to slacken at all, and she kept milking me, trying to get more from me. I didn't know if I'd be able to come again right away, but as long as I was still hard, I would continue to pound away at her for as long as she could take it. . . .

30

Lupe stayed the night, as Lisa had done also, and when we woke we lay there together with our legs entwined, while I idly fingered the nipple of her right breast.

"With you, it is as it should be," she said. "You give great care to giving pleasure as well as taking it. That is very rare in a man."

I didn't know what to say to that, so I simply replaced my finger with my tongue, swirling it around and around until the nipple swelled to incredible hardness. I then moved onto her left breast and repeated the process. While doing that, I slid my hand down between her thighs and dipped my fingers into her wetness. Her hand found my penis and stroked it to its full hardness, and then I was in her again and it was as good as it had been the first time . . . and the second time . . .

This was what Lisa would be like with a little more experience, I realized, and Lisa was what Lupe had been like at nineteen. It was if I had known two women, but they were the same one.

She stroked the back of my hair and said, "You

are a very rare man, Clint Adams. We are lucky,
my daughter and I, to have such a man for a
friend, and to have had you as a lover."

"It is I who am lucky, Lupe, and honored," I
said.

"I must go," she said, sliding her legs from the
bed. I watched her as she dressed, and it was as
erotic a performance as that of the night before,
when she had undressed, only now she was completely unaware of the effect she was having on me.
Even though we had just finished making love, my
penis twitched at the sight of her.

"I must start breakfast," she said, when she
was fully dressed. "You will come to eat?"

"In a little while, Lupe," I promised.

She stroked my cheek and I kissed her palm,
and then she smiled and left.

I lay back down on the bed and clasped my
hands behind my head. We had not slept all that
much, but still I felt invigorated, exhilarated.

It was incredible. . . . She was incredible.

I stood up, stretched until my bones popped,
and then cleaned up and got dressed. I wanted to
go over and check in with Pete, to see if Boyd and
his friends had stirred at all during the night. After
that, I'd go over to Lupe's café for breakfast, and
say good morning to Lisa.

Lupe and Lisa were an uncommon pair, all right.

I began to fantasize, then, about how it would
be to be in bed with both of them—at the same
time!

Two women at once was enough of a fantasy, but
mother and daughter?

I shook my head, trying to clear it of fool notions, but that was one notion that wouldn't clear all that easily.

31

"They didn't move at all?" I asked Pete as he closed the door behind me.

"Not a peep. I'm starting to wonder about those guys, Clint," he said, making a face.

"Well, we won't have to wonder for long," I said. I told him about Leighton's visit to my room the night before, and what his plans were.

"Well, at least he was smart enough to ask for help," Pete remarked.

"Yeah, but he's going to be dumb enough to brace Nelson Boyd right in the street," I said. "That's got to lead to gunplay."

"That might be the answer to all of this," he said, shrugging. "You can't stop it, you know. We established that, already. You can't be a nurse-maid to a man who wants to die."

"Maybe so," I said. "but I want to live and I'm starting with a big breakfast. Come over to the café with me?"

"And leave these three beauties alone?" he asked.

"Nothing's going to happen until after breakfast," I assured him. "I think Dale will make sure I'm around before he braces Boyd. Come on, let's eat."

"You're the boss," he said, grabbing his hat.

We went to the café and Lisa served us two large breakfasts after bidding us both good morning. She smiled broadly at me after she brought us our food, and flounced happily away.

Not only were mother and daughter an uncommon pair, the love they must have felt for each other was awe-inspiring. How many women do you know who would willingly share a man, and here were mother and daughter, doing just that.

And I wasn't complaining.

"That young lady certainly likes you," he said. "What are you gonna do if she wants you to meet her mother?" he asked, kidding.

"I've already met her," I said. "She's a nice old girl."

"Are there wedding bells in your future?" he asked.

"Don't get cute," I told him. "Don't even say that kidding around."

"Been stung, huh?"

"I came close once or twice, years ago," I said, "and that's as close as I want to come. Now eat your breakfast."

We both did, and when all of the food was gone, I asked Lisa for another pot of coffee.

"Okay," I said, when she brought it and left, "I take Sideman and you take Able, right?"

"That's the way we divvied them up," he agreed.

"Right."

"Just one thing," he said.

"What?"

"Are we taking them out of the picture for good, or just for Leighton's play?"

"Just be on him. If he goes for his gun, you can have him," I said.

"All right. Now what if Boyd takes Leighton?"

"Why does that worry you?" I said. "As you said before, that could end the whole thing."

"Sure, but when he sees that we've taken his friend out of the play, won't he want one of us?" He leaned forward and said, "Which one of us gets him?"

I stared at him and said, "You want him, don't you?"

"Nels Boyd? Yeah, I think that idea kind of appeals to me."

"He's yours, then," I said, "and you're welcome to him."

"Well, that's pretty decent of you."

"Don't mention it," I said. "You're the guy who knows all about wanting to die, aren't you?"

"You don't think I can take him?" he asked.

"Can't say," I answered. "I haven't seen him or you, and I really wouldn't care if I never did."

"It doesn't appear that you'll be that lucky, does it?" he asked.

"No," I agreed, "it doesn't, thanks to Dale Leighton."

"Your friend."

"A stranger," I corrected him.

"What does that make me, then?" he asked.

I stared at him, and then said, "I'm tempted to tell you that you're a young fool, but you'd probably prove it by going for one of those pretty guns of yours."

"I never go for one, when I can draw both,"

he said, demonstrating by freeing both guns from their holsters and holding them negligently in his hands.

"Put those things away," I said.

"Come on," he said. "Let's see yours."

"Pete, I don't pull my gun unless I mean to use it, and you'd be smart to do the same."

I said it with such coldness that his face lost all expression and damned if he didn't reholster his weapons.

"I think I'd better settle the check and we'll go and check on Leighton and Boyd and his boys."

"Sure, sure," Pete said, "but remember, depending on how everything goes, Boyd is mine."

He said it with such eagerness that for a moment I just sat there and stared at him.

"Pete, I get the impression that you'd like to see Boyd kill Dale Leighton, because that would free you to draw on Boyd."

"I'll let you in on a little secret, Clint," he said, "and I don't often admit this, even to myself."

"What's that?"

"I like using these guns," he said. "You probably can't understand that, can you?"

"More than you know," I said. "I felt that once, also, a long time ago—until I killed my first man."

"Yeah," he said, examining my face. "I guess you might have, at that."

"Look, Pete, if it turns out that Boyd kills Leighton, and then he kills you, I hope you don't expect me to face him on your behalf," I said.

"But, Clint," he said, spreading his hands, "what else are friends for?"

32

When we left the café, Pete went to look for Boyd and his boys while I went over to Dale's office.

"And try and keep those guns in their holsters," I told him.

"Don't worry," he said. "I'll only take them out for Nels Boyd."

"That's what worries me," I said.

"Aw, Clint, are you worried about me?"

"What else are friends for?" I said, and started for the marshal's office.

Dale was seated behind his desk, holding his gun between his knees and loading it.

" 'Morning, Dale," I said.

He looked up and said, "Hello, Clint. I'm just getting this thing ready for business. Give me a few seconds."

I watched while he loaded the gun without missing a beat, almost casually. I had to give the man credit, and maybe take some for myself, because I'd started him on the road back to being a whole man, even with one arm. The problem was, he'd gotten off my road and onto one of his own.

Once he had the gun fully loaded he closed the loading gate and slipped it back into his holster.

"Okay, now I'm ready," he said, standing up.

"Why don't you give Boyd and his friends time to have breakfast?" I suggested.

"When I'm done with him, it ain't gonna matter to him whether he's eaten or not," he answered.

"What if it comes out the other way around?" I asked.

He shrugged his shoulders and said, "What if it does? That's a chance we take, right?"

"That may be right, but it's not a chance that we *have* to take," I replied.

"Look," Dale said, pointing his finger at me. "Today I'm gonna show something to you, and to this town. Up until now, I haven't faced anyone with a rep, but after I kill Nels Boyd, then *my* rep as the One-Handed Gun will be made."

He was serious, and I probably could have talked myself to death trying to change his mind. Maybe it was time for me to accept my guilt, give up on him, and move on.

"But you might have a point," he added, to my surprise.

"And what's that?"

"Maybe I should let him have his breakfast first," Dale said. "Why don't you go over and recommend the café to him. He'll have some good feed, and one of the last things he'll ever see is Lisa. Could I be kinder to the condemned man?"

"You want me to—" I started, but I stopped myself short and started again. "Dale, I'll back your play to the hilt, but don't expect me to carry your messages and invite a man to his possible death." I started for the door and turned back to him with my hand on the knob. "I'll be out on the street for the next couple of hours," I told him. "If you're going to do this crazy thing, then get it over with, or you might find yourself alone out there, facing not one man, but three."

I left before he had a chance to remark, closing the door behind me with a bang. As I stepped down off the boardwalk, I saw Boyd and his two friends turn the corner onto the main street and walk in the direction of the café. A few moments later, Pete Blue turned the same corner, saw me and stopped.

We both stood where we were and watched them to make sure they were going to the café. When they did enter, I pointed to the café and he nodded. We both stepped down off the boardwalk and headed that way.

I was thinking that maybe we could keep this thing from ever getting to the street.

33

We met in front of the café, and I turned slightly to look back at Dale's office. He was standing in the open doorway, staring across the street at us, his right shoulder against the doorway, his left thumb hooked into his gunbelt.

"What's happening with Leighton?" Pete asked me.

"He's going to wait until they finish breakfast, then brace Boyd as he comes out."

"That's nice of him."

"Listen, I'll go in first, you come in behind me and stay by the door."

"What are you gonna do?"

"I'm going to sit down and have a cup of coffee with them," I said, "and give them some friendly advice."

He stared at me for a moment, then slowly shook his head and said, "Let's go."

I went through the doorway and saw that there were about three tables out of a possible twelve that were occupied. I located Boyd and his pals at a table to my left, already having started on a pot of coffee. As I walked towards them, I heard Pete step into the café behind me.

There were four chairs at the table where Boyd and the others were waiting for their breakfast. I just pulled the fourth chair out and sat down, bringing surprised glances from all three.

"I don't remember inviting you to breakfast with us, stranger," Boyd said, staring at me with light gray eyes. He was somewhere between Blue's age and mine, while the other two were a little older than him. Still, he was the spokesman, the man in charge, and that much was obvious.

"I invited myself," I said.

"Then you better just uninvite yourself," he said. "Eating with a stranger upsets my stomach."

"Then I'll have my say and leave before your food comes," I proposed.

He considered my proposition and then said, "Take three minutes, and then you better be on your way out."

"You're here for Leighton, aren't you, Boyd?"

"So you know who I am," he said.

"Oh, I know who you are, all right," I told him, "and I know why you're here."

"Why's that?"

"You're here to kill Marshal Dale Leighton. Somebody from this town hired you to kill Leighton."

"Leighton," he said, "is that the one-armed lawman who runs this town?"

"That's him," I said.

He shook his head and chuckled, saying, "If that don't beat all. A one-armed man with a whole town under his thumb."

The other two men also laughed, as if on cue,

and when he looked at each one in turn, they fell silent.

"Look, I only came in here to give you some friendly advice," I said.

"Is that so?"

"Yeah."

"Well, you still got one minute," he said, "so you better get to it."

"Leave Leighton be," I said. "Get on your horse and ride out now."

"Before I eat breakfast?"

"If you stay to eat breakfast, it may be the last thing you ever do," I told him.

"I guess this Leighton must be pretty fast with that one hand, huh?" he asked.

"I don't think any of us ought to stay around to find out," I said. "Aside from that, he's a lawman. You kill him and you're going to have every other lawman in the country looking for you."

"You know who I am," he said, "so you know that it wouldn't be the first time the law was on my tail."

"Stay alive, Boyd," I said. "Leave town."

"Can't," he said.

"Why not?"

"Here comes my breakfast," he answered, nodding his head. I turned and saw not Lisa but the plain-looking waitress bringing three plates of steaming hot food.

As she set down the plates of food, Boyd fixed me with a steady look and said, "That's it, stranger. Your time is up. I'm sure me and my friends appreciate your concern, but right now we'd like to eat our breakfast."

I couldn't talk them into leaving, that much was obvious. The only other thing I could have done was brace them right there and then myself, which would lead to someone getting killed. One of them, or Pete Blue, or Lisa, or the other waitress, Lupe or, yes, even me. The last did not concern me as much as the others did, but I stood up and said, "I hope you'll remember that I tried to warn you, Boyd."

"Sure, friend," he said, not looking up from his plate.

I stood there a moment longer, but when none of them looked up again, I slid back my chair and walked over to the doorway, where Pete was standing.

"Hey, friend," Boyd called out behind me.

I had been about to speak to Pete, but instead I turned to see what Boyd wanted.

"Who was it that was trying to warn me?" he asked. "I'd like to know who I owe."

"Adams," I said. "My name is Adams."

"Adams," Boyd repeated, then he shrugged and went back to eating his breakfast.

"Why didn't you tell him your first name?" Pete asked.

"Tell him yours," I said, and walked past him.

Pete followed me out onto the street, and we both saw Leighton, still watching the doorway from his office.

"Clint, maybe if you told him who you were, he'd listen to your advice," Pete offered.

"Yeah, and maybe he'd go for his gun right then and there," I countered, "which is just what I'm trying to avoid."

"Sometimes I think you'd like to live in a world without guns," he said.

I looked at him and said, "You're right, I would. I'd love to live in a world without guns."

"Why would that make a difference?" he asked. "Men would just find some other way to kill each other."

I stared at him again, then shook my head slowly and said, "Damn, Pete, you're a smart young fella, aren't you?"

34

"All right," I told Pete, "if Sideman and Able are going to back Boyd's play, there will have to be one of them on either side of the street. Cross over, and just wait and see what happens. Whoever crosses over will be yours, okay?"

"Sure, fine with me," he said. "I only hope that Leighton appreciates what we're doing for him."

"We'll only have to worry about that if he's still alive when it's all over."

"Good point," he said. "I'll see you later."

He crossed over and stood a couple of doors down from Dale's office, in a doorway. I walked about three doors down from the café and took up position there.

We waited that way, the three of us, all with our own private thoughts. Dale was probably thinking about killing Boyd, which would start him off on his way to his big reputation.

Pete Blue was probably also thinking about adding to his rep, but by killing Leighton or Boyd, whichever survived.

I was still trying to figure a way to keep anyone

from getting killed, but just like in Abilene, that was a physical impossibility when you had so many men who lived by the gun all together in the same town.

Something was going to have to give, and the heavy tension in the air testified to the fact that it was just about to.

I studied the street on both sides as far as I could see. I was looking for anyone who looked as if they knew what was about to happen, but it was still early and the streets were virtually empty. I could see Mayor White's general store, but he was nowhere in sight.

I felt almost certain that the man—or woman— who hired Boyd would have to be there to watch. Maybe I wouldn't be able to pinpoint their identity, but I hoped to narrow it down some.

Finally, it looked like things were about to get underway. The door to the cafe opened and Sideman stepped out. He gave the street a brief look, then crossed over to the other side and took up position leaning against a post.

Next, Able came out, gave the street the same scant look, then moved towards me. For a moment I thought perhaps he was heading for my doorway, but he stepped into the one just before mine.

The last man to step out from the café was Nelson Boyd, who did so patting his full stomach contentedly.

Dale didn't waste any time. He stepped out into the street and called out to Boyd in a loud voice. He wanted his shouting to bring out some witnesses, so that when he killed Boyd, there would be people around to talk about it.

"Nelson Boyd," he shouted.

Boyd glanced across the street and from his left profile I could see that his face was expressionless. Time to go to work, and Boyd was a professional.

"Nelson Boyd," Dale shouted again, "step out into the street. This is Marshal Dale Leighton."

Boyd stood where he was for a few minutes, probably wanting to make Dale wait.

Dale didn't mind waiting, though. If gave him more time to build an audience, and his efforts were paying. People began to look out their windows, and step outside to see what the commotion was all about. I kept my eyes on the general store, and eventually saw Luke White peering out his front window.

"Come on, Boyd," Leighton said. "We have to have a talk."

"What about?" Boyd called back, finally answering.

"Step into the street," Leighton said.

Boyd took a couple of steps, and then dropped down from the boardwalk to the street. Dale moved forward a few steps, and they faced each other across the street.

"What's on your mind, Marshal?" Boyd asked.

"You are, Boyd," Leighton said. "I'd like to know what you're doing in my town."

"Your town?" Boyd laughed. "You sound like you own it."

"That's right."

"I thought you were supposed to be working for the people," Boyd said.

"We have a different arrangement here in Palmerville," Leighton answered.

"Well, I heard about your arrangement,"

Boyd said. "I figured maybe I'd come and see for myself. From what I hear, the people in this town ain't too happy about your 'arrangement.'"

"They don't have to be," Leighton said. "I think you and your friends better ride out of my town, though, if you have any regard for your health."

"You running me out, Marshal?" Boyd asked.

"I mean to," Leighton answered.

I was watching Able, who was one doorway in front of me, standing with his hand on his gun. I glanced across the street, and Pete was in a similar position, watching Sideman.

"Well now, Marshal, I'm afraid that don't suit me," Boyd said. "See, I just had me a fine break-fast in this here café, and it was so good I thought I'd stick around for a couple of days."

"I'm glad you enjoyed your meal, Boyd," Leighton said, "because if you don't get your horse and ride out, it's going to be your last."

Boyd shook his head and said, "Can't do that, Marshal. I think you're gonna have to run me out yourself."

"I'll run you into the ground," Leighton said, and I saw Boyd's shoulders stiffen.

"Man might think you were calling him out, Marshal, talking like that," he said.

"Just move out into the middle of the street, Boyd," Leighton said.

Boyd moved first, and he went to his right. That would mean that Dale would have to go to *his* right, which would put his back to both Sideman and Able. That made Boyd's plan pretty clear, and sullied his reputation a little.

I watched as they both walked out into the center of the street, and then I stepped out and moved up behind Able.

"Take your hand off your gun, friend," I told him, "nice and slow."

Able stiffened, hesitated a moment, then moved his hand away from his gun.

"Now look across the street," I instructed him. He looked and saw Sideman standing with Pete Blue's guns sticking out of his back.

"Your friend, Boyd, is on his own this time, Able," I said. "This should be interesting."

Now we all settled back to watch the outcome, as did everyone else in town who had responded to the commotion. Even Lupe and Lisa had come out of the café to watch.

"If you make a move for your gun at any time," I said to Able, "you'll be dead before either of them is. Understand?"

He nodded jerkily, saying, "I understand, friend, I understand."

"Good. Let's watch, now."

Both Leighton and Boyd had completed their journey to the center of the street and were now facing each other.

"I'll tell you what, Marshal," Boyd said. "If you'll unpin your badge and drop it into the street, I'll let you walk away."

Leighton didn't answer. Instead, he let his gun speak for him. He went for it as soon as Boyd was finished speaking, and I could see the surprise in Boyd's eyes. He had expected Leighton to talk more, or at least let him go for his gun first. I saw the panic in his eyes as he looked over at Able and saw me standing behind him.

Desperately, he grabbed for his gun, but he was way too late. Dale's first shot took him high in the chest and spun him around. The second shot caught him as he was spinning and threw him to the ground where he kicked up a cloud of dust. He kicked his feet some for a few seconds, but then he lay completely still.

"That's it," I said to Able. "Get your friend across the street and ride out, before I change my mind."

He didn't have to be told twice, and when I looked across the street and nodded to Pete, Sideman also took off. Both men were heading for the livery, and we watched to make sure they wouldn't change their minds.

When they turned the corner I stepped into the street and started walking to Dale, who was now standing over the body of Nelson Boyd.

As I reached him Dale looked at me and holstered his gun, saying, "He never even got to his gun."

"He expected more talk from you, Dale," I said.

"What happened to his friends?" he asked.

"Oh, they decided to leave town for health reasons," I said.

"Just as well," he said. I thought he might have meant that it was just as well because he didn't want to have to kill them, but then he said, "Just as well, there would have been no profit in killing them. They didn't have the rep that Boyd did."

"No," I said, looking down at Boyd, who had died with surprise on his face, "I guess not."

"I guess this shows everyone in this town," he said, "and I guess it pretty much showed you, too, didn't it?"

When I didn't answer he looked at me and said, "What did you think?"

"I think you combined quick thinking with a quick move and came out on top . . . this time."

"Yeah, I figured he'd expect me to give him the first move, but once I got to the middle of the street I was through talking."

"You had your audience by then," I said.

"Yeah, that I did," he said, looking around. "I guess there were enough people here, weren't there?"

"There were plenty," I told him.

"I'd better get some of these good citizens to clean up the street," he said. "Did you see Amanda around, by the way?"

"No," I said, looking around again, "I didn't see her at all."

"Too bad," he said. "She missed it."

"Yeah," I said, "she missed it. I'll see you later."

"Thanks for the backup," he said.

"Sure."

As he began shouting for some men to carry the body to the undertaker's, I turned and headed back down the street. Pete Blue had stepped into the street and was walking towards me.

"Where are you going?" I asked.

He had a very serious look on his face as we reached each other and stopped.

"That was impressive," he said.

"Yeah, it was," I said. "So?"

He looked *at* me, then *past* me, and I knew what was on his mind.

"Don't do it, Pete," I said. "Not now."

"What's the matter with now?" he asked.

"He's riding high, now, but the word hasn't spread yet," I said. "If you mean to take him to add to your rep, you'll have to wait for the word to spread, won't you?"

"And what if I was hired to take him?" he asked.

I shook my head.

"You weren't," I said. "You're just young and in a hurry to add to your reputation."

"Look, Clint, you're up there with Hickok already," he said. "You've got your rep, it's easy for you to talk—"

"That's right," I said, grabbing his right arm, "and it should be just as easy for you to listen. Figure I know what I'm talking about, and that it might do you some good to listen."

He was still looking past me at Leighton, then flicked his eyes to catch mine.

"All right," he said. "I'll listen."

"Let's go get a drink," I said.

As we started for The Last Chance I breathed a sigh of relief. True, I had never seen Blue's move, but I had now seen Dale Leighton's, and I had to figure that I had just saved Pete Blue's life.

35

"You don't think I can take him, do you?" Pete asked me over a bottle of whiskey.

"I don't know, Pete. I can't say."

"But you've seen his move."

"And it was a damned good one, but he also used his brain, as well as his hand," I reminded him.

"Yeah," he admitted. "Boyd must have thinking the way I was, that Leighton would give him the first move. I was almost as surprised as Boyd was when Leighton pulled his gun."

"Leighton's been around a few years more than you have, kid," I reminded him.

"Yeah, but now I know," he said. "I won't wait to be offered the first move, I'll take it."

"Did you hear anything I told Boyd in the café?" I asked.

"Sure."

"You want to be hunted for killing a lawman?"

"Come on, Clint," he said. "You've been in this town long enough. What kind of a lawman do you think Dale Leighton is?"

"That don't matter," I said. "He's still wearing a badge, he's still a lawman, even if he's no longer a good one."

"This town would be a damned sight better off without him," he said.

"I can't argue that," I said, "but I still want to try and get him to *walk* away from it, not get *carried* away."

"If you and him ain't friends," Pete said, "I'd like to see the way you protect a friend."

"Maybe I'm trying to protect you right now," I said.

"I don't need it," he said, pouring himself another drink. "I've got these two guns to protect me."

"Why do you need two guns to kill a man?" I asked him. "If you can't do it with one, you shouldn't be wearing one."

He frowned at me, and then said, "All right, I'll take one off."

"That's not what I meant," I said. "If you're so confident, why wear two?"

"I like to wear two," he said, resisting my efforts to try and instill a little self-doubt in him. He laughed then and said, "To tell you the truth, I can't decide which hand I'm faster with, so I wear two."

Cocky and confident, just like a lot of young gunmen before him. Just like Dave Morgan, Dale's old deputy, but he had found out that you need more than confidence.

"I'm going to talk to Leighton again," I said, standing up.

"I'll come with you."

"You're a little unsteady now, Pete," I told him. He was unsteady because I had drunk very little of the bottle, hoping he'd take up the slack, and he had.

"I think even you will admit that you should wait until you're completely sober before trying to face anybody."

He frowned, then said, "Yep, you're right there, Clint, pal. I think I'll just sit here and finish the bottle, then go and take a little nap."

"Good idea."

"Good idea," he repeated. "You don't need me anymore today, right?"

"Right. Go take a nap. It'll be the best thing for you."

"I'll go and take a nap," he said, then laughed and said, "right in the whorehouse. This town got a whorehouse?"

"I don't know," I said, "but if it does, I guess that's where I'll find you."

"Yep," he said, pouring out the last of the whiskey, "that's where you'll find me—but don't come looking too soon, now, hear?"

"I hear," I said, patting him on the shoulder.

At least that would keep him out of trouble for a while.

36

"You don't want me to kill the kid, that's it, isn't it?" Dale asked me a few minutes later. "Percy Blue, right?"

"That's part of it, yeah," I admitted. "But Dale, I don't want you to kill anyone, and I don't want anyone to kill you. The fact that Boyd was here because someone hired him should tell you something. This town is no longer a safe place for you to be."

"You've got that wrong, friend," he said. "When I find out who hired Boyd, this town is not going to be a safe place for that person to be."

"So, then what happens?" I asked. "Somebody else hires another Boyd and it starts all over again."

"I'll take them all," Leighton said, opening a drawer and taking out a bottle of whiskey. "Drink?"

"No, thanks."

He pulled the cork with his teeth and poured himself a drink, then set the bottle down. He finished the drink, poured a second, then replaced the cork and put the bottle back.

"You saw my move, Clint," he said. "You were impressed, I could tell."

"So? Is it so important for you to impress me?"

"I think I'm as fast as Hickok," he said.

"Don't even think it, Leighton," I said. "Hickok is the fastest man I've ever seen with a gun, and I've seen some fast ones."

"Oh, don't fret so," he said. "I ain't about to go after Wild Bill, but you got to admit, he couldn't possibly be faster than I was out there today."

I just looked at him and shook my head.

"You, then," he said, seeing that I wasn't going to comment. "Was I faster than you?"

"It doesn't matter," I said.

"I was, wasn't I?" he said, grinning. "You don't want to admit it, but I was faster than you. Wasn't I?"

I didn't answer, and I saw the anger start to well up from inside him, anger directed at me, which he had probably been suppressing since I arrived.

"Wasn't I?" he demanded, banging his fist down on the desk top.

"No," I said, watching his eyes to see what his reaction would be.

"You're a liar!" he shouted. "I was too faster than you. Faster then you ever were or ever will be. Admit it!"

"Okay," I said, "I'll admit it. You're faster than me."

"You're lying!" he snapped.

"Which way do you want it?"

"I want you to believe it, damn it!" he said. "I don't want you just to say it, I want you to know it."

"I don't care, Dale," I said, honestly. "I don't care if you're faster than me or not. It doesn't matter to me."

"Well, it matters to me, Mr. Gunsmith," he said, standing up so fast that he knocked his chair over. "It matters one hell of a lot to me, and I'm gonna prove it. That's what I should have done last year, instead of just making you leave town."

"I left because I didn't want a confrontation with you, Dale," I said.

"You left because I knew what you and Amanda were doing behind my back, and because you were afraid of me. Admit it!"

If I admitted it, he would call me a liar, and if I denied it he would also call me a liar.

"I'm gonna show you, Mr. Gunsmith-with-the-reputation," he said, pointing his finger at me. "First, I'm gonna take care of your young friend, and then you."

"I won't draw on you, Dale," I said.

"Why not? Amanda won't care. It's her feelings you're worried about, isn't it? Well, she won't care!"

"I care!" I said. "I don't want to kill you."

As soon as I said it I knew it was the wrong thing to say. He went livid and said, "You can't kill me in a fair fight, Adams, and I'm going to prove it!"

I stood up and said, "There's no talking to you. I can see that now."

"The talking is over," he said, "and don't try leaving town, either."

I turned and walked to the door.

"First Mr. Percy Blue, Clint, and then you. Once I kill you, my rep will be as big as yours ever way. Bigger! I'll be up there with Hickok."

"Have it your way, Dale," I said, reaching for the doorknob. I stopped when I heard his gun cock behind me.

"In the back, Dale?" I said. He didn't answer, and I had no idea what kind of expression was on his face, but I was sure that he had simply drawn the gun in anger, but had no intention of shooting me in the back.

"I'm walking out this door, Dale," I said. "If you want to shoot me in the back, go ahead. That would really make a reputation for you."

My stomach was crawling as I opened the door, stepped through, and closed it behind me without looking at him.

37

"Well, it seems to me that he's called the tune and we gotta dance to it," Pete Blue said.

It was later that evening and we were in Pete's hotel room. He was staring at me from wet, blood-shot eyes.

"Maybe," I said, not convinced.

"Only before we dance, my head's gotta stop pounding," he added.

"That's what you get for drinking so early in the day, kid," I told him. "Did you find the whorehouse?"

"Yeah," he said, looking sheepish, "only I fell asleep."

"Still have to pay?"

"Of course."

"Tsk, tsk," I said. "Shame on you, a young buck like yourself—"

"I don't usually drink that much," he said.

I walked to the window and peered out at the dark street.

"What do we do, Clint," he asked, lying on his bed like a dead man. "Just wait for him to come for us?"

"I can't make that decision for you, Pete," I said. "He said you were first." I turned from the window and said, "If I was you, I'd get my horse and hightail it."

"That's a lie," he said.

"Yeah," I said, turning back to the window, "maybe it is."

"Hey, Clint?"

"What?"

"You saw his move. Can you take him?"

"I don't know," I said. "Maybe."

"Well, you won't get the chance," he said, pushing himself up on his elbows.

I looked at him and said, "What do you mean?"

"I'm gonna kill him," he said, "so you'll never know whether you coulda took him or not."

I stared at him and shook my head.

"When are you gonna do that, Pete?" I asked.

He stared at me through half-open eyes and then dropped back on the bed.

"Soon as I come back to life," he said.

After that he fell silent, and pretty soon his breathing became even and regular. I walked over to check on him, and he was asleep. I had to wonder just how good he was with those two guns, and if his confidence was genuine. It sounded more like false bravado to me than real confidence.

Or maybe it could be called wishful thinking.

I wondered if I would be able to stand by and watch as Dale Leighton and Pete Blue faced each other in the street. Certainly, Dale had a psychological edge, having faced Blue down at the card table, even though he'd had my help. Of course, after having killed Nelson Boyd, Dale's confidence level was bound to be sky high.

All in all, I thought that I had a better chance of facing him successfully than Pete did.

Did I think I could beat him? That wasn't really the uppermost question in my mind. What I was wondering was if I could beat him without killing him, which was dangerous thinking. Going up against a man who wants to kill you, you had damned well better want to kill him, too.

I decided to go and see Amanda. I didn't know exactly what I expected to hear from her that would make a difference.

Maybe I was looking for absolution.

38

It was dark when I knocked on Amanda's door, and she answered clad in some kind of housedress. Her hair was slightly disheveled, but still, had it not been for the depressed expression on her face, she would have been very lovely.

"Clint," she said. "It's late."

"Not that late, Amanda," I said. "I'd like to talk to you. Please."

She looked as if she were going to refuse, but then her shoulders dropped another level and she stepped back, saying, "Come in."

I followed her to the living room.

"I have some coffee made," she said.

"I'd like some, please," I said. She nodded and went off to get it. When she returned, she was carrying one cup and set it down on the table next to the worn chair, where I was sitting.

"I hear Dale killed a man today," she said, sitting on the sofa.

"Yes, he did."

"You come here to tell me about it?"

"No," I said. "I came here to talk about the possibility of my killing him."

She smiled bitterly and said, "You came here to save him, and now you're talking about killing him. Has he finally gone beyond the point of no return?"

"I think so," I answered. "He still thinks we were meeting behind his back last year."

"Does he know about . . . this time?" she asked.

"No, I don't think he suspects," I said, and we both knew how ironic that was. "He's threatening to kill a friend of mine, and then me."

"Can he do that?" she asked. "Can he kill you in a fair fight, Clint?"

"I don't know," I said.

"You have quite a reputation. Dale has been following your career for years. He would show me any newspaper articles that had anything to do with you." Her eyes looked dreamy as she reminisced. "He showed me the very first article that referred to you as 'The Gunsmith.' He was jealous even then, Clint. I think the jealousy has festered all of these years, and losing his arm just made everything boil over." She looked straight at me then and said, "He knows he should be grateful to you for what you did last year. He feels that what you did will give him the chance to best you. He's laughed at the irony of that more than once since last year. Now he's finally going to get his way."

"I've tried to talk to him, Amanda," I said. "I've tried to make him see what's happening to him, but he refuses—"

"Who was the man he killed today?" she asked.

"A hired gun."

"Hired by someone from town?"

"I believe so," I said. "Maybe even Mayor White, himself."

"That wouldn't surprise me," she said.

I remembered the coffee and took a sip, but it had gone cold.

"I don't want to kill him, Amanda."

"Are you looking for permission?" she asked. "All right, then, go ahead and kill him. You have my permission. You will be doing me, the town, and probably Dale a favor."

"I'm not looking for permission," I said.

"Forgiveness?"

I shook my head. 'I don't know," I said. "I don't know what I'm looking for."

"Just ride out, then. Forget it. If you leave, his reputation will grow anyway. He'll tell everyone that he ran the Gunsmith out of his town for the second time."

"And then somewhere down the line he'll get a bullet in the back," I said.

"So?" she asked. "You don't want to kill him, so somebody else will. What's the difference."

"Dignity," I said. "No man should die from a bullet in the back fired by a coward. That's an obscene way to die."

"Obscene?" she asked, staring at me. "I don't understand you men. *Dying* is obscene, not the *way* you do it, but *doing* it! There's no good way to die."

"A man deserves to die seeing the man who pulled the trigger," I said. "Facing him in the street, with an equal chance to kill him."

"You're as crazy as Dale is," she said, standing up. "Go ahead, face him in the street. Kill or be killed with *dignity,* but I'll not mourn either one of you."

She stalked from the room and I watched until she disappeared. I thought about what she said about dying, and disagreed. There was no shame in dying honorably.

I don't know, maybe I learned something from that short conversation with Amanda, something about myself, and other men like me. Like Bill Hickok, Wes Hardin, Ben Thompson, and all the others who lived by the gun. In doing so, they assured that they would die by the gun. They—we—had chosen how we preferred to die the day we picked up our guns. That was why we traveled around the country, wearing a gun on our hip, sitting with our backs to the wall. We knew how we wanted to die, and by God, that was the way we'd do it. With dignity.

Dale Leighton deserved to die with dignity, no matter what kind of a man he had become. And me? If he killed me instead, well that was the way I chose to die.

I stood up and left Amanda's house, knowing now what had to be done, and knowing a lot more about myself than I had known in years.

39

I stormed into Luke White's store the following morning and asked him, "Did you enjoy the show yesterday?" He stared at me and so did the lady he was waiting on. "Of course, it didn't quite end the way you planned, did it?"

"Look, Adams, can't this wait—" he began, but I cut him off.

"No, it can't wait," I said.

He looked at the woman then and said, "Mrs. Bradley, could you come back a little later, please? You understand, I'm sure."

If she did, she didn't show it. She just stuck her nose in the air and stalked out. He followed her to the door, closed it and locked it, then turned to face me.

"All right," he said. "I admit it. I hired Nelson Boyd to get rid of Marshal Leighton. For God's sake, Adams, I had the welfare of my town in mind."

"You know," I said, "Leighton talks the same way. 'My' town. You both think that this is your town, but you're both wrong. This town belongs to the people of Palmerville."

"But they have placed its welfare—and theirs—in my hands," he argued. "I have a right to do what I have to do to protect this town from men like Dale Leighton."

I opened my mouth to reply, but I couldn't argue against what he had said. He was the Mayor, and the welfare of the town was in his hands.

"You do have a right to protect the town," I said, "but hiring a gunman was not the way to do it."

"Then you tell me how to do it," he said. "I'm open to any suggestions."

"Look," I said, coming up with an idea that I should have thought of before, "I was a U.S. marshal for a long time. I have some connections. Let me see who I can talk to about having Dale Leighton, uh, retired."

His face brightened and he said, "Do you really think you can do that?"

"I don't think anything," I said. "In fact, it might even be too late for this."

"What do you mean?"

"Never mind," I said. "I'll send somebody to Cheyenne with a message," I said. "Somebody has to be told the way he's abusing his authority."

"Adams, if you can get this done, the whole town would be very grateful to—"

"All right," I said, holding up my hands to stop him, "forget that. Just let me do what I can, and promise me you won't hire any more guns."

"I'm finished with that," he said. "I'm at my wits' end, and if you can do something . . ."

"I'll let you know what happens," I said.

"Thank you," he said, "thank you for . . . understanding."

"Yeah, well, I'm understanding a lot of things lately that I never could before."

I left him there, probably feeling as puzzled as I did, myself.

I only hoped I hadn't come up with the idea too late to save some lives.

40

There was one sure way of getting a message delivered, and that was to hop on Duke and take it to Cheyenne myself. However, I was afraid of what I might find when I returned.

The other way was to have someone else deliver it. . . .

There was only one person in town I thought I could trust to do that, but could I get him to do it? I went over to Pete Blue's hotel to see if he had come to life after a night's sleep. As I started up the stairs the desk clerk said, "You looking for your friend?"

"Yeah," I said, stopping a few steps up. "Is he in?"

"Nope. He went out earlier, and hasn't come back yet," he answered.

I came back down and walked to the front desk.

"Do you know where he went?"

"Nope. I don't keep tabs on all my guests," the man said.

"The marshal hasn't been by today, has he?"

"Leighton?" the clerk said. "Geez, I hope not. I can do without having him on my back, thanks."

"Yeah, okay. Thanks."

"Just thanks?" he said, looking at me expectantly.

I reached across the counter, put my hand on his shoulder, winked and said, "Thanks."

"Thanks a *lot*," he said.

I checked the café first, but Lisa told me that Pete hadn't been in for breakfast.

"Do you want me to make you something?" she asked.

"No, honey, I don't have time now," I said. "Maybe later."

Where else was there to look? There were a couple of other places he might have gone to eat, and then there was the whorehouse. Or the livery stable.

Suddenly it struck me. I felt sure I knew where Pete had gone, and I hoped I would be able to catch him in time.

41

He was right where I thought he was, with his horse saddled and ready to go. He was seated on a bale of hay, holding his horse's reins in his hands, and he was deep in thought.

"Pete," I said, and his head jerked up.

"Oh, Clint," he said. He looked at the reins in his hands, and then back at me.

"I guess you know what I'm thinking," he said.

"I believe I do, yes," I said.

"I guess I'm not as confident as I thought I was," he admitted.

"I think there's something more important than confidence, Pete," I told him.

"What's that?"

"Honesty," I said. "You've got to be honest with yourself. If you don't think you can match Dale Leighton's move, then going out on that street would be suicide."

"Running is cowardly, though," he said. "Are my only choices suicide or cowardice?"

"No. I think I have another alternative."

"What?" he asked, standing up. "If you knew

how long I've been sitting here, trying to decide whether I should stay or go . . ."

"I think you should go," I said.

"You do?"

"Yes . . . right to Cheyenne."

He frowned and asked, "Why there?"

"I want to send a message to the Federal Building," I said. "I want to try and get Leighton removed from office."

"Do you think you can?" he asked.

"If I can get a message there fast enough," I said. "You could be there and back by nightfall—if you'll do it."

"Do you think that'll make a difference?" he asked.

"It just might get this town out from under his thumb," I said.

"Depending on who the new marshal ends up to be," Pete said. "Leighton won't take this lying down."

"I guess not."

"Are you looking for the job?" he asked.

"Not me," I said. "I stopped wearing a badge a long time ago."

"Clint," he said, "you're setting the new marshal up for a showdown with Leighton."

"No," I said, "I'm not doing that at all. The Leighton problem will be solved before he gets here. Will you make the ride?"

"Sure," he said. "It still means I'm running, but at least my running will accomplish something."

I gave Pete the message to deliver, and then gave him the name of a judge in Oklahoma to use as a reference.

"He'll vouch for me," I said. "Tell whoever you speak to to send him a telegram and check up on me."

"I hope he takes your word for it," he said.

"At the very least it'll start an investigation, and there are enough people in this town who will tell an investigator everything he needs to know."

"I can believe that," he said. He pulled his horse around and mounted up.

"Thanks, Clint," he said.

"For what?"

"For giving me a direction to go in," he said. "For understanding."

That was the second time in one day someone had thanked me for being understanding.

"Just ride, kid," I said. "Deliver that message and then go . . . wherever you want to go."

"No," he said. "You said I could be there and back by nightfall, and I will. I promise you that."

I watched him ride out, and hoped that he would be able to keep that promise.

42

After Pete left town safely—and I watched him until he faded from sight—I found that I was hungry and went to the café for one of Lupe's breakfasts.

When I arrived at the café I told Lisa, "One of your mother's big breakfasts, please, Lisa."

"Coming up," she said, and hurried off to get it.

Over my *extra*-large breakfast, I realized that though I may have solved the town's problem, mine still existed.

Leighton still wanted to prove that he was faster than I was. Maybe once I had him removed from office, I could leave the matter of Dale Leighton to the new marshal, but that wouldn't have been fair. After all, I did create the problem, so it was up to me to dispose of it.

I couldn't let Dale kill any more people with a skill that I had helped him develop. At last, I decided that if he wanted to face me, then I'd face him. . . .

But not until he was stripped of his badge.

As Lisa came to the table with another pot of coffee she stopped short, looking at the front door.

I turned and saw Dale standing there, looking at me without much of an expression on his face.

"Go ahead, Lisa," I told her, "put the coffee down and go into the back room."

"Yes, Clint," she said. She did as I said, and then I turned to Dale and said, "Come on over and have a cup of coffee, Marshal."

He looked slightly surprised at my invitation, but he walked over and pulled up a chair.

"What are you trying to pull, Clint?" he asked.

"What do you mean?"

"You got the kid to ride out of town, didn't you?" he asked.

"So?"

"I don't like that," he said. "I had plans—"

"Dale," I said, interrupting him, "I really don't care much what you like and what you don't."

"Is that so?"

"Yeah, it is," I said. It occurred to me that if I changed my tack with Dale, I might slow him down a little. With Pete Blue gone, he might be in a hurry to get me to step into the street with him. However, if I showed him that I wouldn't mind facing him, that might just make him sit back and think—long enough for the order stripping him of his authority to come.

"You realize that without him around, it's just you and me," he said.

"I know that," I said. "That's why I got rid of him."

"What do you mean?" he asked, frowning.

"He's an innocent bystander, Dale," I explained. "This should only be between you and me."

"You mean, you're willing to meet me, face to face?" he asked.

"Sure, why not?" I asked. "I taught you how to use your left hand, didn't I? Do you really think I have any doubts about being able to outdraw you?"

He got angry.

"You're damned well right I think so," he said. "You're afraid of me, admit it!"

"We'll see who's afraid of who when we're out in the street, Dale," I said. That could have either prompted him to call me out right at that moment, or caused him to back off, which was what I wanted. We matched stares for a few minutes while I waited for him to make his decision.

Finally he stood up and said, "I'll tell you when that will be, Adams. You sweat it for a while. You just sweat it."

With that he strode out of the café and I sat back and let out a long breath. Now it all depended on Pete Blue. I hoped he would be convincing enough for someone in Cheyenne to help us out. And I hoped he'd have the courage to come back and let me know what had happened.

Lisa came out hesitantly and then walked to my table.

"Is he gone?"

"He's gone," I assured her, "and pretty soon, he may be gone for good."

43

It seemed doubtful that Dale would call me out that day, so I felt—for the first time since coming to Palmerville—that I could just relax, while waiting for Blue to return.

I took the opportunity to ride Duke around some, and then brushed him down when we came back and spent some time just talking to him. Horses have feelings, too.

After that I went over to The Last Chance to try and find a poker game. I felt sure that Dale wouldn't come walking into there interrupting the game. Hickok had a favorite saloon in Abilene—The Alamo—and Dale Leighton had his favorite in Palmerville—The Red Bull. And there the similarity ended, no matter what Dale thought.

I found three fellas in the saloon who didn't mind playing, but the stakes were small, and after a while I started to lose interest. After losing a few hands in a row because of boredom, I left the game and the saloon.

I went by the café and found that it was relatively slow. I asked Lisa if she was busy, and she immediately knew why I was asking and said that she wasn't.

While we were in bed together I started to fantasize about having her mother there with us. I had never had two women in bed with me at once, and the prospect was very exciting. What made it even more exciting was the fact that they were mother and daughter.

With Lisa lying in the crook of my arm, resting, I wondered if she and her mother would ever agree to that, or if they would be shocked by the proposal.

I began to idly play with the nipple of her right breast and she pressed her body against mine, running her hand between my legs.

"You are always ready," she said, flicking at the head of my penis with her thumb.

I didn't tell her that I was ready because I had been thinking about her mother. Instead, I covered her mouth with mine to keep her from asking any questions and then positioned myself so that, without preamble, I could drive myself into her, at the same time driving the breath out of her.

"*Dios . . .*" she moaned as I began to work myself in and out of her in long, deep strokes. She wrapped her legs around my waist and I cupped her tidy little bottom in my hands. She was built along the same lines as her mother, but her body was not as full in the breasts or the buttocks. I was not complaining on either count, however. I fitted inside each woman just right, and that was what counted.

Afterward, while she was again resting in the circle of my right arm, she said, "Will you be leaving soon?"

"I hope so," I said before I could stop myself. She pouted and I tilted her head up with my fingers beneath her chin and said, "You and your mother are probably the only good things that have happened to me in this town."

"You are sad, then?" she asked.

"Yes," I said, "about a few things."

About the change in Amanda, which probably made me ever sadder than the change in Dale. Of course, the change in Dale had brought about the change in his wife, and again I realized that much of the change in Dale was due to me. Still, Amanda was the one who had asked me to come and "help" him. I guess the blame pretty much could have been shifted from head to head very easily. Maybe I was taking too much of it upon myself.

"What will happen between you and the marshal?" she asked.

"Probably what we both knew would happen all along," I said, only I hoped he would no longer be marshal when it did finally happen.

Of course, when he lost the badge it remained to be seen what effect that would have on him. Maybe it was the shock he needed to bring him back to his senses. It was too late, in my opinion, for him to patch it up with Amanda, but maybe he'd abandon this "One-Handed Gun" business when he was no longer marshal of Palmerville and go on to live a normal life.

"If you kill him what will happen to you?" she asked.

"I don't know," I said. And I didn't want to think about it. I turned to her and put my hand over her breast.

As I massaged her breast she asked, "God, are you ready again?"

I was always ready with Lisa, especially with the

image of her mother in mind as well. We made love again, just as eagerly as the first time. Lisa prepared to leave shortly after that, to help her mother with the dinner rush.

"Will you be coming for dinner?" she asked.

"I don't know if I can walk that far," I said, kidding with her.

"This was your idea," she reminded me.

"I'm not complaining," I assured her. "If I get hungry, the café will be my first stop," I promised.

She smiled, kissed me, and left.

Outside it was starting to get dark, and I wondered if Pete had run into any difficulty. Maybe they hadn't taken him seriously. Maybe nobody there had heard of me or, worse yet, maybe they remembered only one part of my reputation—the wrong part. I had been a damned good lawman while I wore a badge, but it seemed all people ever remembered was my ability with a gun.

I decided there was no point in worrying about Pete until morning; chances were he'd decided to stay overnight in Cheyenne to give himself and his horse a chance to rest up. This day was gone, darkness was falling, and Dale wasn't going to call me out in the dark. So okay, Pete could have until tomorrow morning. I didn't think Dale was going to wait that much longer—I didn't think he'd be able to. I had backed him up a little bit earlier that day, but that wouldn't last long. Even now he was probably wishing he had called me out right there and then.

The more I thought about it, the more sure I was that he'd be out in the street early the next day, calling out my name as he had called out for Nelson Boyd.

I stood up and began to get dressed because suddenly dinner in the café, served to me by Lisa and cooked by Lupe, did not seem like such a bad idea.

44

After dinner I grabbed a bottle of whiskey and brought it back to my room with me. I didn't have a chance to talk to Lupe, or I would have asked her to come to my room after she closed. I didn't feel right about asking Lisa to give her such a message, and I didn't ask Lisa to come because it wasn't fair to her to be in bed with her while thinking of her mother.

I pulled a chair over to the window of my room and put my feet up on the windowsill. I started working on the whiskey bottle, and before I knew it, I was awakened by the sunlight streaming through the window and into my eyes.

I had slept the entire night in that chair, and it hadn't been the whiskey, because the bottle was still three quarters full.

I guess I must have been just plain tired.

I grabbed some clean clothes, went downstairs and into the back of the hotel, where they had their bath facilities.

On my way back to my room from the bath, I stopped at the front desk and asked the clerk if I had any messages. I was hoping that maybe Pete had returned during the night and left me a note, but that wasn't the case.

"No messages, Mr. Adams," the clerk said.

"Thanks."

I left my dusty, slept-in clothes in my room, tucked the Colt New Line inside my shirt, and then went to the café for breakfast. I decided that I would force myself to have a nice, leisurely breakfast before I walked over to the other hotel to see if Pete had checked back in.

I ate my breakfast while watching the door, waiting for either Pete or Dale Leighton to walk in. By the time I finished my food, neither of them had shown up.

"More coffee?" Lisa asked.

"Of course," I said.

When she brought me my second pot of coffee, somebody finally came in the front door, but it wasn't either of the people I was expecting.

It was Amanda Leighton.

She spotted me right away and came over to my table, obviously agitated about something.

"Clint, I've been looking for you," she said, breathlessly.

"Sit down, Amanda," I said, "and catch your breath."

"I went to your hotel," she said, taking a seat, "and they told me you usually eat here."

"Do you want a cup of coffee?" I asked. Lisa was waiting patiently to see if we needed an extra cup.

"No, I didn't come here for coffee," she said. I shook my head at Lisa and she walked away.

"What's on your mind, Amanda?" I asked. "I

was pretty sure you said all you had to say the last time we talked."

"I'm sorry about that, Clint," she said, "I really am. I haven't been myself."

"No," I agreed, "you haven't."

"Listen, Dale came to see me last night."

"He did? What did he want?"

"He told me that today was the day he was going to kill you," she said. "And he meant it."

"I believe he did."

"You have to leave town."

"Why?"

"Why?" she asked. "Because I don't want to see you get killed, that's why."

"Well, that's nice to hear," I said.

She knew what I was referring to and lowered her eyes.

"I know what I said, but I didn't mean it."

"What about Dale?" I asked. "Would you care if it was him who got killed?"

"I . . . don't know, Clint, but I don't want you to think about that. I just want you to leave."

"I can't leave, Amanda," I told her. "I've got to see this through. I can't leave the town under Dale Leighton's thumb."

"Are you just going to wait for him to call you out?" she asked.

"I've sent a message to Cheyenne," I said. "I've asked them to remove Dale from office."

"Do you think they will?" she asked.

"I don't know, but at the very least they should send an investigator out here, or a judge, to see for themselves."

"Oh, I hope so," she said. "I hope so for the sake of the town."

"What are you going to do, Amanda?" I asked. "Are you going to stay here?"

"I'm already packed, Clint," she said. "I'm going East, no matter what happens. I've had enough. I have some relatives back East, and I'm going to stay with them for a while."

"That's probably the right decision for you," I said.

"I'm sorry I can't say the same for you," she said.

I poured myself some coffee and said, "I'm partly to blame for this whole thing, Amanda."

"And I've got the other part of the blame," she said. "I asked you to come here, which started the whole thing."

"It has to end, Amanda," I said. "One way or another, it has to come to an end."

"I suppose you're right," she said.

"When are you leaving?" I asked.

"There's a stage this afternoon," she said. "I'll be on it."

I put my hand over hers and said, "Good luck."

"You, too," she said. "I'm sorry it all had to be this way."

Suddenly, from outside, we both heard Dale Leighton's voice call out, "Adams! Clint Adams!"

Her eyes widened and she said, "Oh, my God."

"I know you're in the café, Adams!" Dale shouted. "Come on out and face me!"

"Don't go, Clint," Amanda said. "He'll kill you."

"I've got to go, Amanda," I said, standing up. "Stay inside."

"Adams!"

I didn't answer, but I started slowly for the door.

45

I stepped out onto the boardwalk and located Dale Leighton, standing across the street. When he saw me he smiled a tight, ugly smile and stepped down off the boardwalk.

"It's time, Clint," he called out to me.

"Let's get it over with," I replied. "I got other things to do."

I said the last part loud enough for the people on the street to hear, and Dale stiffened at the insult.

"You'll have nothing else to do after this, Adams," he replied. "Move out into the center of the street."

We both started to circle to our right and kept walking until we reached the center of the street.

"Wait!" somebody yelled.

Dale's head snapped around in the direction of the voice, but I kept my eye on him, knowing he'd take every advantage he could get, as he had done with Nelson Boyd.

"Hold on!" the voice shouted, closer this time. It was the kid, Pete Blue.

"Well, well," Dale said, "it looks like your

friend wants his turn after all."

Pete stepped down off the boardwalk into the street as I looked over at him. He was holding a piece of paper in his left hand.

"I have a message here for Clint Adams from Cheyenne," he said aloud, holding the piece of paper aloft.

"What the hell is this?" Dale demanded.

Pete walked over to me and handed me the piece of paper while Dale and the townspeople watched.

"Where were you?" I asked.

"I got in last night and registered in your hotel," he said. "Read that. I think you'll be happy," he said.

"You want me to face both of you?" Dale was shouting. "Is that it? Neither one of you wants to face me alone?"

I read the message Pete had brought me, then looked up and scanned the streets, trying to find the face I wanted among the people lined up to watch one of us kill the other. Finally, I located the man I wanted.

"Mayor White?" I called out.

White stepped hesitantly from a group of people and said, "Yes?"

"Would you come over here, please?" I requested.

He looked at Dale, who was appearing more puzzled by the moment, then stepped into the street and walked over to Pete and me.

"Mayor, this is a message from Judge Wilson in Cheyenne," I told him. "It gives me full authority as an investigator for the Federal Marshal's Office to study Marshal Leighton's actions and do as I see fit. That means I can let him stay in office, or remove him from office and strip him of all authority as a U.S. marshal."

"May I see that?" White asked.

I passed it over to him and he read it. He then turned around and, holding the paper above his head, announced, "Dale Leighton is no longer marshal of Palmerville."

In the midst of the townspeoples' cheering, Dale shouted, "You're crazy!"

"This paper gives Clint Adams here the authority to remove Leighton from office," White went on.

"I don't recognize that authority," Dale shouted.

"Well, as mayor of Palmerville, I do!" White retorted.

"Let me see that," Dale demanded.

"Give it to me," I said to White, and he handed it over.

I started towards Dale with the message and he stood his ground, watching me warily, his hand hovering near his gun.

"Take it easy, Dale," I said. "I'm just going to show this to you."

"Give it here," he demanded, sticking out his hand. I reached him and handed him the message.

"It's official," I said. "You are no longer marshal of Palmerville, Wyoming. Give me your badge."

He threw the paper to the ground, said, "Like hell I will," and started to reach for his gun.

I was close enough to him so that I was able to grab his hand before he could pull his gun.

"Let go," he said.

"After I take this," I said. Using my other

hand I removed the badge from his chest.

"You're finished, Dale," I said. "It's all over."

"Let go of my hand," he said from between clenched teeth.

"I'm going to let go and walk away," I said. "You shoot me in the back and you'll be a murderer. You are no longer the law in this town, Dale. You can't just call somebody out in the street anymore and get away with it. The rest of this message says that the new marshal will be here tomorrow." I took my hand off of his and said, "I suggest you be gone by then."

I bent over to pick up the piece of paper he had dropped, and then turned and started walking away from him.

"Clint, watch it—" I heard Pete Blue shout. I saw Pete go for his gun and then heard a shot from behind me. The bullet caught Pete and spun him around, dumping him on the ground.

I went down on one knee, drawing my gun, and turned to point it at Dale. His gun was trained on the fallen Pete Blue, but his eyes were on my gun.

"Drop it, Dale," I said.

"No way," he replied.

"Put it down or I'll drop you," I told him.

"No you won't, Clint," Dale said, smiling at me. "You'd like to, but you won't. I'm going to holster my gun, Clint, and then you are going to back off and holster yours. Either that, or you'll have to kill me now, just like this, because I'm not putting my gun down. I'm going to show all of these people just who is faster, you or me."

"Don't be a fool," I told him. "Dale, I've

known all along that I can beat you. Don't make me prove it to you."

"You're a liar!" he snapped angrily. "I'm holstering my gun, Clint. Back off and do the same, and I'll show you."

It was the only way to really end it. Our roles were suddenly reversed. Although I wasn't a U.S. marshal, I did have certain authority granted me by the message Pete had brought with him, so I was the one who was official, and not Dale, but that didn't seem to bother him.

"All right," I said. "All right, damn it, I guess this is the only way to end it."

I started to back away, watching him the whole time, but he went ahead and cleanly holstered his gun. I backed off a few more steps, and then holstered mine.

This was it, then.

I continued to back up a few steps, watching Dale closely, and then called out behind me to Mayor White.

"How's the kid, Mayor?"

There was a moment's hesitation, and then he answered, "He's alive," and that was all.

I had no doubt but that Pete Blue had saved my life. Dale would probably have shot me in anger had Pete not gone for his gun to protect me. In doing that, he became the immediate danger to Dale, who switched targets and shot Blue.

I had to be satisfied with that answer for the moment, however, because I had more pressing matters to deal with.

I had a man to kill.

"That's far enough," Dale said to me. "Don't

be worrying about the kid, Clint, because after I've finished with you, I'm gonna kill him, too."

"You're crazy, Dale," I said, "and I'm sorry—"

He made his move then, as I had expected. As soon as he started talking to me—something he had not done with Nelson Boyd—I knew what his plan was. Engage me in conversation, and then when I was answering him, he'd draw his gun and kill me.

It didn't work out that way.

I watched as his hand streaked towards his gun and sure enough he was very fast.

He was not, however, anywhere near as fast as he thought he was, and he realized that as my bullet pierced his chest. I could see the realization in his eyes as his mouth dropped open and he staggered back from the force of the bullet.

When he fell to the ground, his gun was still in his holster.

46

When the new marshal, Max Tanner, arrived the following day, I turned over the badge I had taken off Dale Leighton, and explained to him everything that had happened the day before.

"I'm sorry it had to end that way, Adams," he said, seating himself behind his new desk. "From what you tell me, it all sounds as if it were on the up and up."

"You can ask anybody, Marshal, starting with the mayor," I told him. "I had no choice."

"I accept that," he said, "although I will have to ask some questions. Why don't you plan on staying in town one or two more days?"

I had been planning to leave that day, but I agreed to wait a day or two.

Tanner was a big man, young for a marshal, I thought, but he appeared to be competent.

"I'll wait to hear from you," I told him.

"Fine," he said. "I shouldn't be too long."

I turned to leave his office and he asked, "Oh, how was the boy who got shot trying to help you? Pete Blue?"

"Percy Blue," I said, correcting him. "He died this morning."

"Oh, I'm sorry."

"Yeah," I said, opening the door, "so am I."

The doctor had told me that the fact that Blue had made it through the night was a near miracle. The bullet had done massive damage, and by all rights Percy Blue should have died on that street.

"He must have wanted to live very badly," the doctor told me.

"I guess we all do, Doc," I said. "Thanks for trying."

From the doctor's office I had gone to see Tanner, and now I walked over to the café.

Amanda had left on the stage the day before, refusing to claim Dale Leighton's body. She said that the man who had died in the street was not her husband. Dale was buried that same evening in Palmerville's version of boot hill.

As I reached the café, I decided to change my direction and I headed for The Red Bull Saloon. I thought I needed whiskey more than I needed coffee.

Whiskey and sadness make for a lot of lost hours, or so I had heard. Now I proved it. . . .

I woke up the following morning and thought that maybe I had been dreaming. Hadn't I gone to see the new marshal in the morning, the day after Dale was buried? What was I doing here in bed . . . and whose bed?

I looked around and realized that I wasn't in my own hotel room. In fact, it didn't even look like a hotel room. While I was still trying to decide where I was, the door opened and Lisa came in, carrying a pot of coffee.

"Good morning," she said.

"What time is it?"

"It is morning," she said.

"I know that, but it was just morning yesterday . . . wasn't it?"

She put the coffee down on a table by the bed and then put her hands on her hips and stared down at me with an amused look on her face.

"You men," she said, "you insist on drinking as much whiskey as you can, and then you wonder where yesterday went."

Yeah, I remembered buying a bottle of whiskey—or maybe more than one bottle. And I remembered being miserable.

And now it was the next day.

"Where am I?"

"You are in my room," she said, "above the café. My mother and I brought you here when you came to the café last night."

"Your mother—" I said, trying to remember. "I guess I must have been pretty drunk."

"You were drunk," she said, smiling, "but you were not that drunk."

"What do you mean?"

"You told my mother and me that you wanted to do something you had never done before," she said.

"I *did?*"

Smiling, she nodded.

"And what was that?"

"You do not remember?"

"No, I don't."

She shook her head and gave me an exasperated look.

"You said that you had never been to bed with two women at one time, and you said that doing it with a mother and a daughter at the same time was very exciting to think about."

Oh Jesus, I must have been drunk, I thought, closing my eyes.

"I guess you and your mother must have been pretty shocked, huh?" I asked.

"We were not too shocked to enjoy it," she said. "Drink your coffee, it will make you feel better," she added, and then she walked to the door and was gone before I could stop her.

"What?" I said aloud, to the walls.

I looked around me, as if searching for some proof of what she had just told me. Both of them?

I couldn't have forgotten that, could I?

Epilogue

Marshal Tanner had asked all his questions and gave me the go-ahead to leave that same day.

I had given up on trying to force myself to remember the night before, and hoped that somewhere down the line, it would all come back to me. I also started to wonder if Lisa and her mother weren't just having some fun at my expense.

In spite of the charms of Lupe and Lisa, I was not at all reluctant to leave Palmerville. I had learned some things while I was there, especially about myself, and maybe that was good. But for the most part my time in Palmerville was best forgotten.

Which wasn't very likely.

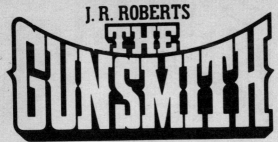

J. R. ROBERTS
THE GUNSMITH

SERIES

J.D. HARDIN

**"THE MOST EXCITING
WESTERN WRITER SINCE
LOUIS L'AMOUR"**
—JAKE LOGAN

_____	0-872-16840	BLOOD, SWEAT AND GOLD	$1.95
_____	0-872-16842	BLOODY SANDS	$1.95
_____	0-872-16882	BULLETS, BUZZARDS, BOXES OF PINE	$1.95
_____	0-872-16877	COLDHEARTED LADY	$1.95
_____	0-872-21101	DEATH FLOTILLA	$1.95
_____	0-872-16911	DEATH LODE	$1.95
_____	0-872-16843	FACE DOWN IN A COFFIN	$1.95
_____	0-872-16844	THE GOOD, THE BAD, AND THE DEADLY	$1.95
_____	0-872-21002	GUNFIRE AT SPANISH ROCK	$1.95
_____	0-872-16799	HARD CHAINS, SOFT WOMEN	$1.95
_____	0-872-16881	THE MAN WHO BIT SNAKES	$1.95
_____	0-872-16861	RAIDER'S GOLD	$1.95
_____	0-872-16883	RAIDER'S HELL	$1.95
_____	0-872-16767	RAIDER'S REVENGE	$1.95
_____	0-872-16839	SILVER TOMBSTONES	$1.95
_____	0-867-21133	SNAKE RIVER RESCUE	$1.95
_____	0-867-21039	SONS AND SINNERS	$1.95
_____	0-872-16869	THE SPIRIT AND THE FLESH	$1.95
_____	0-425-06001-2	BIBLES, BULLETS AND BRIDES	$2.25
_____	0-425-06333-3	BLOODY TIME IN BLACKTOWER	$2.25
_____	0-425-06337-2	THE MAN WITH NO FACE	$2.25
_____	0-425-06151-5	SASKATCHEWAN RISING	$2.25
_____	0-425-06248-1	HANGMAN'S NOOSE	$2.25